'It's an exceptional woman who can laugh at herself like that,' Rory stated thoughtfully.

'Huh! If you really want to know, I felt more like ending it all at first. How stupid can one get?'

'I didn't think you were stupid. Well, not exactly. A little confused perhaps . . .'

'Don't push your luck,' Robin advised, lips twitching again. 'It's as much your fault as mine if I did get confused. Who ever heard of a doctor taking a physio on a home visit? It never happens at St Crispin's.'

'Dear me, we are put out,' he reckoned in a soft, beguiling voice, such as he'd never used to her before. 'Would it help if I told you I'm beginning to understand why my partners approve of you the way they do?'

Drusilla Douglas is a physiotherapist who has written numerous short stories—mainly for Scottish based magazines. Now the luxury of working part-time has provided her with the leisure necessary to embark on novels. *The Vallersay Cure* is her second Doctor Nurse Romance, the first being *Surgeon in the Highlands*.

THE VALLERSAY CURE

BY

DRUSILLA DOUGLAS

MILLS & BOON LIMITED
ETON HOUSE   18-24 PARADISE ROAD
RICHMOND   SURREY   TW9 1SR

*First published in Great Britain 1989
by Mills & Boon Limited*

© Drusilla Douglas 1989

*Australian copyright 1989
Philippine copyright 1989
This edition 1989*

ISBN 0 263 76484 2

*Set in Times 10 on 11 pt.
03 – 8907 – 58794*

Typeset in Great Britain by JCL Graphics, Bristol

Made and Printed in Great Britain

GLOSSARY

Vallersay—Isle of Mountains (loosely from the old Norse)

GAELIC

caileag — girl
cailleach — old woman
bodach — old man
mo ghaoil — my dear
mo gràdh — my love
céilidh — party

Bratanport   (loosely)   the place of the salmon

CHAPTER ONE

TOWARDS the end of the crossing, and in spite of the weather, one passenger put on her mac and went out on deck. Robin Maxwell leaned over the rail and peered forward into the damp grey mist, but the Isle of Vallersay remained obstinately hidden. June it was—yet quite nasty enough for March. Such a disappointment, having seen herself arriving on one of those gorgeous sunny days of cherished childhood memory. Only this time, she had come to Vallersay to work.

It had been a tremendous surprise to her when the Health Board appointed her, on references alone, by return of post. Not so to the physiotherapist-in-charge at St Crispin's. Delighted and grateful to get somebody from a world-famous London hospital, that was how she saw it. 'Your new colleagues will be quite overawed and very much on the defensive,' she predicted, 'so all your tact and understanding will be called for, Robin dear, but I know you won't be tempted to drop your standards.'

'I won't, Miss Cavendish.' Robin felt quite able to promise that, though doubtful of causing anything like the stir her superintendent expected.

After a preliminary crackle or two, a lilting Highland voice came over the loudspeakers inviting drivers to be going below now, as they would be reaching Bratanport in five minutes chust. Robin waited for the stampede of eager holiday visitors to subside before making for the steep companionway that led down to the densely packed car-deck. Having located her car, she frowned at the clock as she slid behind the wheel. Just fifteen minutes to get to her meeting and she didn't even know where the new Health Centre was.

She asked the boy who was collecting the tickets, and with true island curiosity he asked her why she wanted to know. Robin smothered a smile and told him solemnly, 'I'm the new physiotherapist.'

His eyes widened. 'Iss that so? And we were hearing it wass a man that wass coming.' With a glance of warm approval, he added, 'I am thinking that you will be a ferry nice surprise.'

'That's awfully kind of you,' she returned, dimpling. 'But the Centre . . .?'

'Iss at the foot of the hospital brae. Turn right when you get off the boat and chust you keep going. You cannot miss it—so grand and fine it iss—not at all like anything else in Vallersay.' He moved off after a final appraisal, leaving Robin to chuckle over the mistake about her gender. With an interchangeable name like hers it happened all the time and she had given up minding when she was still at school. Come to think of it, the secretary at the Health Centre had made the same mistake when typing the senior doctor's letter; a thought which set Robin wondering what her new boss would be like. Rather pompous, judging by the tone of his letter. Elderly then, set in his ways and miles behind the times. She was going to need all that tact Miss Cavendish had praised.

Robin's turn to disembark came at last and she joined the line of cars bumping carefully over the ramp and trundling down the cobbled pier. The mist was much less dense on land, and her spirits rose as she recognised the sameness of the buildings clustered at the pier-head of the island's only town. Vallersay—her enchanted isle of happy memories that was going to make her forget.

Two minutes' drive along the sea front brought Robin to the Health Centre. Even softened by the thinning mist it was still hideous. All glass and concrete, it squatted like a vulgar relation below the dignified little hospital of red sandstone. Hopefully it would weather in a year or two—all the builders' paraphernalia in the car park suggested it wasn't quite finished yet.

There was nobody at Reception or in the entrance hall-cum-waiting-room and Robin searched fruitlessly up and down the wrong corridor before finding a door with Dr McEwan's name on it. Out of nervousness, she knocked more imperiously than she meant to. The door was opened by a tallish, broad-shouldered man in jeans and a checked sports shirt. He had a screwdriver in his free hand and Robin took him for one of the workmen. 'I wonder if you can help me?' she asked with a polite little smile. 'I'm looking for Dr McEwan.'

'Dr McEwan is on holiday and morning surgery is over,' he explained in the gentle accents of the islander. 'What were you wanting?'

Robin bit her lower lip in perplexity. 'That's awkward,' she said, disregarding all but his first words. 'Dr McEwan told me to report to him here as soon as I landed.'

The man had been looking at her as if he didn't at all mind what he saw. Now he frowned. 'Just who are you?' he asked carefully.

Robin controlled her impatience. 'As it happens, I'm Miss Maxwell, the new physiotherapist, and, as he wrote to me to meet him here this morning, Dr MacEwan must be somewhere about, so if you have any idea where I can find him . . .' she stopped, harebell-blue eyes darkening with disapproval. What did the man mean by staring at her with such obvious dismay?

He stood aside and motioned her into the room. 'You've found him,' he said heavily. 'I am Dr McEwan.'

'G-good morning,' she breathed, dropping weakly into the chair he indicated. Where was the pompous old man who had written to her? Pompous for sure, but this Dr McEwan was young—hardly more than a year or two into his thirties, and with a plentiful thatch of rather untidy brown hair in place of the silvering fringe she had given him in imagination. Narrowed grey eyes continued to survey her mercilessly from a tanned, outdoor sort of face that was rugged rather than handsome.

Caught off balance like this, Robin found it hard to meet his scrutiny and shifted her own to his unorthodox outfit. Hardly the thing for a first meeting with a new colleague, she would have said. But then he is supposed to be off duty, she reminded herself.

'As I told you, I am still officially on holiday,' he said, reading her expression aright and making her blush. Having achieved that, he dropped easily into the swivel chair by his desk, long legs stretched out in front of him and hands clasped loosely across his stomach. If this was how the boss behaved, what in the world could she expect of the others? And it didn't go with his attitude. Ah, well—Robin sat up very straight and primly crossed her ankles to let him see that she knew what was what. With a small sigh of resignation he revealed, 'We were expecting a man—which would have been much more suitable.'

Robin sat up even straighter, determined not to be disconcerted. 'I can't see why—unless all the patients are giants,' she returned quietly. 'I'm sorry to be a disappointment, but there isn't anything I can do about it.'

He allowed his eyes to wander unhurriedly over her from head to toe, resurrecting her blushes. 'I have to agree with that,' he concluded. 'You are certainly very—feminine.' He sat up straight and folded his arms with decision. 'So there is nothing for it but to welcome you to Vallersay, Miss Maxwell.' The way he said it left no doubt that the belated greeting was a duty, not a pleasure.

'Thank you—that is very kind, Dr McEwan,' Robin responded with gentle irony. 'I'm very glad to be here.'

'Are you?' he asked with the merest lift of an eyebrow. 'I wonder why?'

He had managed to disconcert her three times in about as many minutes and Robin hoped he wasn't going to keep it up. 'Well, I have spent many happy holidays on the island and now I look forward to—to living here,' she concluded in a rush.

'I've spent many happy holidays in the Swiss alps, but I wouldn't choose to live there. Come now, Miss Maxwell. Why did you pick on Vallersay?'

Robin certainly wasn't going to tell him that! 'I just got tired of the pace and stress of London and wanted a complete change,' she offered instead.

'Indeed?' She could tell he didn't believe her. 'You've certainly achieved that, but how long will it be before you feel the need of another change, I wonder? Young women in their mid-twenties seem to prefer cities to remote Scottish islands. But then perhaps you have particular friends here?'

A pity she couldn't have said yes to that, instead of having to admit, 'Er—no.'

He shrugged. 'Of course you are quite entitled to keep your own counsel, Miss Maxwell, but I assure you my question had a firmer basis than idle curiosity. Having been without a physiotherapist for eight months, we were hoping for somebody with a valid reason for settling here. A married man would have been ideal. Also, the post calls for considerable experience— probably more than you have. As the only physio, you will have to cope with any and every condition, you know.'

Too young, of doubtful commitment, the wrong sex and not sufficiently experienced. Anything else? Robin swallowed an angry retort because on one count, he certainly had a point. She hadn't come to Vallersay intending to stay for any longer than it suited her. So how was she going to deal with all his doubts? 'You are—very frank, Dr McEwan,' she began carefully, 'and I take your point about wanting somebody permanent. I can't promise to stay for ever, but I will stay as long as I'm enjoying my work. And that will depend on others, as much as on me,' she added pointedly, glad to note by the tightening of his jaw that he had taken that on board. 'As for my experience, I've covered everything. As a student, I was encouraged to think of teaching some day, so my post-graduate clinical work has been varied to that end. Anyway, the Health Board are satisfied,' she wound up to clinch things—as she thought.

'Ah, yes—the mighty Health Board,' returned Dr McEwan dismissively. 'I would be more inclined to respect their judgement if they had taken the trouble to interview you—or, better still, allow us here to—but they preferred not to go to that expense.' He smiled thinly. 'So here we are with a *fait accompli* of which we must all make the best. You said you'd thought of teaching. Why did you change your mind?'

'Because I came to realise I'd lose nearly all contact with patients,' she answered promptly.

'Quite so, but if they wanted you to teach, then you

must have been a good student. And St Crispin's has quite a decent reputation, so I hope you are now a good therapist.'

Quite decent? Robin felt herself turning purple. She'd taken personal slurs without protest, but no backwoods medic who hadn't made the grade and didn't know how to dress was going to sneer at St Crispin's and get away with it! 'St Crispin's Hospital is one of the foremost teaching centres in the world,' she informed him crushingly.

'If it is, that'll be because half its professors are Scots,' he returned imperturbably, before lapsing into gloom again. 'Of course, there's not the slightest chance that a Sassenach like you has the Gaelic.'

'I'm not English, I'm a Scot, but no—I haven't.' She patted her capacious shoulder bag. 'I've bought myself a phrase book, though.'

A tiny flicker of amusement softened his face for a fleeting second. 'Very thoughtful, but some of our patients have no English at all.'

'A lot of the patients at St Crispin's were immigrants,' she retorted crisply. 'If I can make myself understood by Chinese and Indians—and Arabs, then surely I can get through to my fellow Scots.'

Now she was sure he had smiled. 'Only time will tell if your confidence is justified,' he observed wryly, as he got to his feet. 'Now, I'm going to show you round the Centre before taking you up to the hospital. That way, neither of us will waste valuable time when you start work on Monday. Come along.'

Obediently Robin followed him out into the corridor, where he waved a hand towards three closed doors. 'My colleagues' rooms,' he said. 'We are four altogether and we've spent more than the required time in hospital, so we can cover most run-of-the-mill problems between us.

Dr Drummond is a qualified anaesthetist, Dr Anderson
is an obstetrician and Dr McLeod was a consultant
physician in Edinburgh until a myocardial infarction
forced him into semi-retirement. I'm a surgeon. Not
quite the backward rural set-up you had been expecting,
perhaps?' he asked with a flash of insight.

'I had assumed that an island with three thousand
people on it would have a—a fairly comprehensive
medical team,' she improvised; rather creditably, she
felt, at such short notice.

'Beautifully put,' he returned, undeceived. 'Now let's
look at the rest.' He threw open doors on treatment,
records and store rooms with bewildering speed before
coming at last to Physiotherapy. 'Your domain,' he said
shortly, standing back to let her enter.

It was larger than she'd expected and seemed to be
very well equipped, though it was difficult to be sure
with half the stuff still unpacked. 'We didn't try to
arrange things, thinking you would rather do that
yourself,' he said, again as if he'd read her mind. Had
he got the second sight? Robin hoped not. That would
be too much to take on top of all the disapproval.

'I shall come in and sort everything out
tomorrow—so as not to waste time on Monday,' she
added, quoting his own words back at him.

'Just what I was going to suggest myself,' he
answered coolly. 'Now for the hospital.' He led the way
back to the entrance where he locked the doors behind
them and handed her the keys. 'Your set—and for
heaven's sake don't lose them,' he instructed.

As if she would! Robin made a tremendous business
of stowing them safely away in an inner pocket of her
bag. This Dr McEwan gave every promise of being as
much of a trial as the one she had pictured.

The Health Centre was built on hospital ground and,

disdaining the longer route by the drive, Dr McEwan embarked with the easy stride of the hill-walker on a path that led steeply upwards through a thicket of wild rhododendrons. After recent heavy rain, the path was muddy and treacherous, and Robin in her light court shoes had difficulty keeping up with him. Realising this, he slowed down a fraction. 'London pavements and fancy shoes are not the best training for Vallersay,' he observed maddeningly, then gesturing towards the mist-enshrouded mountains he told her that a few easy walks in the foothills would soon toughen her up.

'If I'd known this interview was going to be so—so testing, I'd have worn my climbing boots,' she muttered grimly. If it was all right to turn up dressed like a mountaineer, then he should have said so in his letter. Which reminded her to tell him firmly that she had first climbed Ben Iolair, Vallersay's highest mountain, at the age of ten.

'Wonderful,' he observed laconically, as they stepped out on to the drive that ran the length of the hospital.

A stout and smiling middle-aged lady in navy blue appeared in the doorway as they mounted the steps. Her smile froze as her astonished gaze lit on Robin. Another who had been expecting a man? Dr McEwan confirmed that in his introduction. 'Yes indeed—our new physio, *Miss* Maxwell,' he stressed. 'Miss Crombie, Senior Nursing Officer.'

'Senior Nursing Officer, my foot,' observed Miss Crombie roundly. 'You know fine that most folk still call me Matron.' Recovered from her initial surprise, she seized Robin's hand and shook it vigorously as she said warmly, 'You are very welcome, my dear. We've been feeling the lack of physiotherapy sorely.' Then she suggested that coffee before going round might be a good idea.

'No thanks, Ella,' declined Dr McEwan calmly. 'I'd rather get on, if you don't mind. I'm going fishing.'

Matron seemed to find this quite in order, but Robin was furious. Of all the nerve! There had been such a crowd on the boat that she'd never got near the snack bar, and she'd have loved some coffee. Getting up at five so as to be here at the time he specified had been no joke. And for what? So that he could go fishing!

He turned suddenly and caught her frowning at him. 'I expect you had coffee on the boat,' he assumed. 'Unless of course you spent the crossing in the bar.'

Robin was cross enough now to tell him she'd quite lost count of all the doubles she'd downed, but Miss Crombie got in first and ticked him off for teasing the poor wee lassie like that. Robin was amazed to see how well a man of his morose temperament could take a telling off. He was actually smiling as he disappeared into a room off the hall.

He came out wearing a crisp white coat and carrying another, which he handed to Robin. 'The smallest we have, but it'll have to do for now.'

'I didn't realise I'd be needing a uniform this morning,' she said as she put it on and rolled up the sleeves.

'Of course you didn't. You're not officially on the payroll until Monday. Right! Ready when you are, Ella.'

There were eight beds in the first room they entered and the first patient Dr McEwan selected was a Gaelic speaker. He's done it on purpose, the brute, thought Robin grimly, running a professional eye over the lady during the unintelligibile exchange. She was also noticing that Dr McEwan had put on more than a white coat. His bedside manner would not have disgraced St Crispin's itself. She was just wondering where he had got it when he said almost gleefully, 'You won't have found any of that very helpful, Miss Maxwell, so I had better tell you all about our patient.'

'First, may I make a guess or two? Chronic bronchitis and probably asthmatic as well, since she's obviously on steroids,' she reeled off before he could agree or not. 'And the collar and cuff sling suggests a fracture of the surgical neck of the right humerus. Quite recent too, judging by the stage of the bruising.'

'Masterly—as far as it goes,' he allowed, while Miss Crombie beamed her approval of such expert observation. 'But you still need dates and other details, do you not?'

'Presumably I can get those from her case notes, Doctor—unless they are in Gaelic,' she added softly.

He ignored that and suggested silkily, 'It would be very interesting to see how you would teach this good lady to increase the depth of her breathing, Miss Maxwell.'

'Certainly,' agreed Robin, setting to work at once using the miming technique she had developed for her non-English speaking patients at St Crispin's.

'Absolutely brilliant, dear,' was Miss Crombie's assessment. 'And I can see that Mrs MacPhail understood it all.' She said something to the patient who smiled and nodded enthusiastically.

Dr McEwan was obliged to admit that Robin's approach seemed to have worked, but he didn't let up. She was required to give her views on the treatment of all twenty patients in the hospital, whether they were for physiotherapy or not. You may think you've been landed with a pig in a poke, she thought as they made their way back to the front door, but you've lost no time in finding out how much this little piggie knows!

'Now then, have you any questions for me, Miss Maxwell?' he asked crisply as he took off his white coat and handed it to Matron.

'Yes, I have, Dr McEwan, but I'll save them for another time as you're in such a hurry.'

He gave her a speculative look, well aware what she was getting at. 'Thank you for remembering I'm on holiday,' he answered coolly. 'But why not see if Miss Crombie can answer them for you? I know she plans to give you your lunch.'

He's got the hide of a rhinoceros, decided Robin, as she watched him plunge back down the rhododendron path after a short exchange with Matron. Meanwhile Miss Crombie was also gazing after him, but in her case with something very like maternal affection. 'We're so lucky to have a man of his calibre here,' she enthused. 'Not many would have given up what he did to come here in the first place—never mind what he's sacrificed to stay.'

That would have got anybody's curiosity going and Robin was willing and eager to hear more, but Matron abruptly changed the subject. Glancing up at the sky she prophesied that the mist would surely have lifted by evening and then she hoped that Robin didn't mind cold tongue and salad for her lunch as this was cook's half-day.

No more was said about Dr McEwan's selfless behaviour, but during the meal in Miss Crombie's little cottage behind the main building Robin did get most of her professional questions answered. When they had drained the coffee-pot between them, Matron in her turn asked Robin where she was staying. On hearing that she had managed to get into a guest house in the town she said, 'Yes, I know the one. Mrs McKenzie, the proprietress, has an excellent reputation. You'll be very comfortable there.'

'Oh, good,' said Robin. 'Unfortunately I can't afford

to stay for too long, though. I suppose there's not much chance of finding a cottage to rent at this time of year?'

Miss Crombie said she doubted that very much but she would let Robin know if she heard of one. 'And now you'll be wanting to get along to Black Rock and get settled in,' she expected.

They parted company most cordially and Robin went away down the hill to get her car, feeling very grateful that she had at least one well-disposed colleague in the Matron.

Black Rock Guest House was on the southern edge of the town, so Robin drove back the way she had come, renewing acquaintance *en route* with Bratanport's main street which fronted the bay. There was the Town House with its curved outside stair, little clusters of old-fashioned shops, the Italian ice-cream parlour—gaudy as ever—the red sandstone kirk with the top-heavy bell tower and, back from the road atop a tiny hill as befitted its status, the imposing and very pricey Royal Stuart Hotel. Stopping at the chemist's to buy toothpaste, Robin was childishly pleased to find the same balding, bespectacled man behind the counter.

The guest house was spruce and sparkling from the bright red geraniums in the hanging baskets all along the veranda to the snowy white lace curtains at the windows. The proprietress, too, was a miracle of neatness, and Robin wasn't surprised to be told how lucky she had been to get a room. 'Now I am full right up until the end of the season,' said Mrs McKenzie, as she led the way up the winding stair.

Robin's room was charmingly old-fashioned with rosebud wallpaper, white furniture and a faded pink carpet. But the large walk-in cupboard in the corner housed a shower and loo. Mrs McKenzie had had to move with the times because, as she said, the visitors

who had been to Spain and other such foreign places
seemed to expect it. Then she pointed to a white
envelope on the dressing-table. 'You'll be noticing that
you have a letter, though why Mrs Anderson should be
calling you Mr Maxwell, I am not knowing. Mrs
Anderson is the doctor's wife and she does part-time as
radiographer at the hospital. Her eldest boy brought it
on his bicycle.'

After such a lengthy description Robin waited for
Mrs McKenzie to tell her what was in the letter but, not
having the second sight like Dr McEwan, she couldn't.
Being quite as curious as her landlady, Robin slit the
envelope open. 'They've asked me to supper tonight,'
she discovered with pleasure.

'There now, and is that not nice? She'll be about ten
years older than yourself, but very lively and cheerful
like all the folk from Glasgow. You'll not be wanting
for good company if Mrs Anderson takes you up.'
Curiosity satisfied, Mrs McKenzie went out, promising
to send the girl Flora up with the rest of Robin's
luggage.

Robin telephoned the Andersons to accept the
invitation—Mrs Anderson declared herself delighted to
discover that the new physio was female—and then she
spent the next two hours unpacking, arranging her
things, having a leisurely bath and washing her hair.
Then, armed with hairdryer and brush, she sat on the
bed with her feet up and considered prickly Dr
McEwan. What a welcome—or lack of it—for
somebody who had come to Vallersay to repair her
battered ego! If he had a bone to pick with anybody it
was with the Health Board—not her. She had very
nearly told him so, too, before prudence intervened.
After all, she had to work with the man. And having
thought of work, surely his prejudice would melt when

she had shown him how competent and energetic she was. And had he honestly thought he was going to get a man, married or single, who would be content to stay indefinitely? In her experience they were all hell-bent on getting to the top, not burying themselves on remote Scottish islands, to borrow his own phrase.

It had been a man who had beaten her to the senior post on Orthopaedics at St Crispin's. Nothing to choose between you, but he has a wife and child to support, had been the unofficial reason to filter through, so perhaps she had an excuse for feeling miffed about Dr McEwan's chauvinistic attitude. It had been bad enough, that damp and dreary April morning, to get the Board's letter telling she'd been unsuccessful in her application. But getting her marching orders from David, just hours later, over a hurried canteen lunch with half the hospital looking on had just about winded her. She had been so sure he was over Marcia. He hadn't turned a hair when they heard that she was coming back to St Crispin's, yet the minute Marcia appeared . . . Resolutely Robin thrust aside the memory of that humiliation. One disaster she might have borne but not two; private and professional lives both knocked for six.

Since Robin had decided there was nothing for it but to leave St Crispin's, it had seemed like fate when she spotted the advertisement for this job in Physiotherapy. Where better to repair her self-esteem than on lovely, peaceful Vallersay? Peaceful? Robin laughed ironically. There wasn't going to be too much peace around an awkward customer like Dr McEwan. One thing for sure, though. Coping with him in the present wouldn't leave much time for brooding about the recent disastrous past.

When her bright milk-toffee-coloured curls were dry,

Robin switched off the dryer and crossed over to the window to lean out. Matron Crombie had been right about the weather. Now Vallersay was looking exactly as she remembered it. The U-shaped bay was an expanse of sparkling ripples broken only by a few yachts riding at anchor. Gentle rolling hills enclosed the town like a collar, and beyond the hills rose the mountains, purple-grey and peaceful against the vivid June-blue sky. Robin leaned out and took some deep breaths of the fresh and fragrant air, before turning her attention to choosing something suitable to wear for the evening.

Since Robin was last in Bratanport, a rash of new bungalows had broken out on the hills behind the town and the Andersons lived in one of the largest. There were already three cars standing on the square of gravel in the angle of the house, suggesting there were other guests. She walked towards the porch, hoping that her bright Liberty cotton skirt and cream blouse would fit the bill. Before she could ring the bell, the door was flung wide by a vivacious redhead who beamed at her and cried, 'I'm Lindsay Anderson and you must be Robin. We're so delighted you could come.' She accepted with unaffected pleasure the bottle of wine Robin had stopped to buy *en route*, then towed her across the hall and into a spacious modern sitting-room, facing the sea. It was full of men, dressed casually in slacks and shirts, and women in cotton frocks, reassuring Robin about her own outfit.

Present were Lindsay's husband Jock, the obstetrician, and the remaining partners in the practice with their wives. The speed at which Lindsay conducted the introductions would have left Robin totally confused, but for the rundown on names and special interests she'd had from Dr McEwan that morning. It was a relief to note that he wasn't there, but then it wasn't likely that a man of his awkward temperament would get on with these charming and welcoming people.

Jean McLeod soon realised how confused Robin was. 'Don't worry, my dear, you'll have sorted us all out by the end of the evening,' she said encouragingly. 'Now tell me, have you even been to Vallersay before?'

'Every year until I was ten. Then the Bank moved Father to their London office and we started exploring England instead.'

Jean being another Scot brought up in the south, they had plenty to talk about until Robin was annexed by the three doctors, who wanted to talk shop. They had all been amused rather than disconcerted at finding out she was a girl, and Robin soon realised there'd be no difficulty about working with them. She had been there for nearly an hour when Dr McEwan strolled casually in through the open patio door. Tonight he was dressed like the other men, in pale slacks and a crisp white shirt, though scorning their neat cravats. Wants to show off his strong bronzed neck, scoffed Robin inwardly, masking her disappointment with a stiff smile when he acknowledged her with a brief nod.

'Damn you, Rory,' cried Lindsay Anderson, hurrying over to him and kissing him warmly on the cheek. 'You've probably ruined the supper. Where on earth have you been?'

He returned her greeting with a careless hug, then brought his other hand out from behind his back to offer her four fat trout dangling on a string. 'Peace offering,' he said. Lindsay shrieked with delight and kissed him again before running out to the kitchen with her prize. Robin reluctantly abandoned the idea that Dr McEwan didn't get on with his partners and their wives.

He accepted a drink from Jock and explained easily, 'The reason I'm late is that I've been doing our Archie's work for him. Old Colin McKenzie's had another of his attacks. They knew I'd be up at the lochan and flagged me down as I passed the croft.' He turned to Dr Drummond. 'I did the necessary, Archie, but it won't do any harm to look in on him tomorrow.' When he smiled at the rest of the company his rugged face was transformed into one of surprising charm. 'I'm sorry I held you up. Are you all starving?'

'Not to worry, man,' reassured Jock. 'We've spent the time very profitably grilling our new colleague here. I doubt the poor lassie's feeling quite fashed.'

Rory McEwan looked at Robin without too much sympathy. 'She'll have given as good as she got,' he assumed. 'Incidentally, did you know you're needing a new offside front tyre, Miss Maxwell?'

Trust you to spot that, thought Robin, clenching her fists tight in the pockets of her skirt. 'I got a puncture while driving up yesterday, so that was my spare wheel you noticed,' she explained.

There were murmurs of sympathy from the others, but all he said was, 'Spare or not, it needs renewing. Punctures are a daily hazard on these roads, so I'd get along to the garage fairly soon if I were you.'

'Oh, I will. And thank you for mentioning it, Dr McEwan,' answered Robin with an exaggerated deference which earned her a long, cool look just as Lindsay came back into the room to announce that supper was waiting.

At the long oak table in the dining-room, Jock showed Robin to the place of honour on his right. 'What rotten luck that was getting a puncture,' he said as they all sat down. 'And you'd be on some deserted moorland road too most likely. At least yesterday was fine.'

'Not on the M1, unfortunately,' revealed Robin with a rueful little smile. 'The rain was absolutely pelting down.'

'Surely you never drove all the way from London to Ardraig in one day?' Jock let out a long whistle.

Robin resisted the temptation to glance at Dr McEwan as she said in a martyred little voice, 'I didn't finish at St Crispin's until after evening clinic on Thursday, so I had no choice. Of course I . . .' she stopped. She'd been going to say she'd intended to stay a night *en route* and catch the evening boat today until she got Dr McEwan's letter, but it was stupid to antagonise him any more. 'I've always loved driving,' she substituted lamely.

Across the table wide blue eyes met narrowed grey ones and Robin knew that if she'd fooled the others she hadn't fooled him. 'When I suggested this morning for our meeting, I was under the impression, thanks to our revered Health Board, that your previous employment terminated a week ago. When you got my letter you had only to phone and we could have arranged something for tomorrow.'

She might have known he would have a reasonable comment to make. 'So it should have been,' she confirmed reluctantly, 'but my replacement was taken ill suddenly and so I stayed on as long as I could to help out.'

'I hope St Crispin's appreciated that as much as we do your epic dash,' he answered calmly—and apparently sincerely.

Then Dr Drummond said they were all very intrigued to know why she had forsaken the hallowed halls of St Crispin's to come and work in their placid little backwater.

Placid indeed! Again Robin resisted the temptation to glance at Rory McEwan as she started on the explanation she had prepared after failing to convince him that morning. 'Despite my English education and accent, I am a Scot,' she began. 'We come from Edinburgh and, as my father has to retire early on health grounds, my parents are moving back there. So,' she gave a pretty little shrug, 'this seemed as good a time as any for me to come back to Scotland too.'

There were murmurs of agreement all round the table, and Hamish McLeod said gallantly that St Crispin's loss must be Vallersay's gain.

'Scotland I can understand, but why Vallersay?' interposed Dr McEwan wickedly. 'There are excellent hospitals in Edinburgh. Why didn't you try there? But perhaps you did,' he added half to himself.

Robin caught the implication all right. Was there no end to his cheek? 'Perhaps I will—if that paragon of a physio you are hoping for ever turns up,' she retaliated, 'but the fact is, this was the only senior post going in Scotland just now that I liked the sound of.' If he asked her why she hadn't waited until something less remote turned up she was done for, but he didn't; just went on staring at her thoughtfully until Lindsay brought in the pudding.

After the meal, Lindsay ordered the men into the kitchen to deal with the dirty dishes, saying she knew fine that was the only way she and the other girls would ever get a chance to talk to Robin. Then she led the women back to the sitting-room. The shadows were lengthening and it was a lot cooler now, so she shut the patio door and put a match to the fire. 'You'll not need fires in June down in London, I'm thinking,' she said to Robin.

'No, but it's a whole lot colder down there in winter, I

suspect,' was Robin's prompt reply.

'Oh, indeed it is,' agreed Netta Drummond, wife of the group's anaesthetist and a part-time nurse at the hospital. 'The year before we got married, I went down to do a post-registration course at the Westminster and nearly froze to death that January.' She embarked on a long and gruesome story about burst pipes, power cuts and chilblains. 'I was never so glad to get back to Vallersay in all my life,' she ended.

'So you belong to Vallersay then,' realised Robin, sitting down beside her on the couch.

'Oh, yes—and so does Rory. We're cousins, by the way.' She smiled and Robin registered a fleeting likeness. 'Being only fourth generation, though, we're still considered incomers by the diehards. Incidentally, half the population of Vallersay is related in some way to the other half, so you'd best bear that in mind, Robin.'

'I will—and thanks for the warning. You said fourth generation . . .'

'Yes. When our great-grandfather came to the island as a young doctor, life here was very hard and primitive. The boats only called once a month so he was very isolated and had to do everything—surgery, babies, dispensing—the lot. I often wonder what he would have made of the glass menagerie.' When Robin looked puzzled Netta explained, 'That's what Rory calls the new Health Centre. His father tried hard to get them to build something more in keeping with the place, but it seems there's a standard pattern that must be adhered to!'

The men rejoined them then and all except for Rory, who must have felt he'd already done his bit that morning, they went on briefing Robin on the various aspects of medicine as practised in Vallersay. It was fascinating and she was grateful, but towards midnight she was having to stifle little yawns as yesterday's marathon drive and her brief night in the hotel at Ardraig caught up with her.

'You're needing your bed, lassie,' diagnosed Jock firmly when he noticed. 'Away home with you now. Have a long lie and a quiet day tomorrow, and we'll all look forward to seeing you on the job on Monday.'

Robin thanked him and Lindsay and everybody else for a wonderful first evening on the island. 'If the patients are as nice as my colleagues, I shall probably stay in Vallersay for ever,' she heard herself saying.

'Very pretty indeed,' observed Rory McEwan—the first thing he'd said for some time. 'You may not have the Gaelic, *caileag,* but you're doing fine in English.'

'I meant that,' she protested frostily, being nearly sure that *caileag* was Gaelic for disagreeable woman, or something like that.

'So did I,' he retorted, which only made it worse.

'Don't you mind Rory's teasing,' said Lindsay, putting her arm round Robin's shoulders when, goodbyes over, she was seeing her out to her car. 'He's a super guy really, but the fact is, things haven't been going too well for him this last wee while.'

'I'm sorry to hear that,' said Robin, feeling faintly remorseful in case she'd misjudged the man. 'Nothing serious, I hope?'

'No, just—well, I'm sure you know how things can pile up,' returned Lindsay vaguely, showing more restraint than Robin would have expected from one so uninhibited.

She murmured something appropriate and probed gently, 'I gathered this morning that my arrival is rather a disappointment, too. Apparently he would have preferred a man—or at least an older woman.'

'That I can well believe,' agreed Lindsay, so promptly as to compound the mystery. 'But don't you worry. He's very fair, and he'll soon come round if you can show him what a super physio you are.'

Robin would have liked to probe further, but doubted she would get anywhere, so she just thanked Lindsay again for a lovely welcome, to be told that she must come again very soon.

Despite her weariness, Robin went straight for her Gaelic dictionary as soon as she got back to Black Rock to find out what exactly Rory McEwan had called her. Not an old woman at all, she discovered, and nothing worse than a girl. The two words were very similar, though, and she had better remember in case she made that mistake again when talking to a patient. Her mind was teeming with many other thoughts and impressions but it had been a very long day and she couldn't stop yawning. Sorting them out would have to wait.

CHAPTER TWO

NEXT morning, Mrs McKenzie took breakfast in bed to her newest guest. As she pulled back the curtains, Robin struggled slowly upright and blinked in the strong sunlight. 'Heavens—what time is it?' she asked drowsily.

'Only ten just,' was the cheerful reply. 'Did you sleep well then, *mo ghaoil*?'

'The best night's sleep I've had in weeks,' Robin realised with surprise. Vallersay's magic must be at work already. 'I'm so sorry I didn't hear the gong, though.'

'There, there—not at all. You'd be gey tired after your journey and then going out. Did you enjoy your evening?'

Robin said yes, that she had very much.

'Aye, they're very hospitable. There'd be others there besides yourself, likely.'

Robin stifled a chuckle. 'Yes, I've met all my medical colleagues and their wives now. At least . . .' She stopped. Maybe it was Dr McEwan's marital problems Lindsay had been alluding to. If he treated his wife the way he seemed set to treat his new physio, then Robin for one didn't blame her for running away or whatever it was she'd done. Her landlady was looking expectant though so she improvised hurriedly, 'I suppose there are just the four doctors in Vallersay?'

'Aye—did they not tell you that? Well, well, they would be too busy finding out all about you, I'm thinking.' Mrs McKenzie took the cover off a plate of eggs and bacon and laughed disbelievingly when Robin said she'd never manage all that. 'Ach, so you will. And now what are you

30

thinking of doing with yourself this fine day?'

'I need to spend some time at the Health Centre, but first I think I'll go for a drive and visit some of my favourite haunts.'

Mrs McKenzie said that was a fine idea and crossing over to the chest of drawers she picked up Robin's thermos flask. 'I'll just be taking this down with me, for you'll be needing a good packed lunch.'

After such a breakfast Robin couldn't believe that, but she didn't say so, realising that Mrs McKenzie prided herself on the scale of her catering.

By eleven, Robin was driving south along a road that turned and twisted with the shore, though separated from it by massed beds of wild yellow irises. Vallersay's abundant wildlife was everywhere. Herons fished in rock pools, oystercatchers filled the air with their anxious cries and seals were basking on the offshore rocks. It was all so beautiful and relaxing it was hard to remember she had come to Vallersay to work. Further on, under the steep cliffs at the south end of the island, small family groups were dotted about on the famous beaches. She had come here so often with her parents and their friends, the McKnights, who lived here then. The father had been in the bank in Bratanport and there were two children—a boy and a girl. Her best friends for three weeks every summer, but Robin hadn't seen them for years.

In response to a strong wave of nostalgia, Robin parked the car on the springy green machair, took off her sandals, and went barefoot over the silver sand to paddle in the cool clear water. Giggling children splashed her as she went along and, laughing, she splashed them back. Then, realising that there might be some islanders among the holiday visitors on the beach, she put on a sober expression and went back to the car. From now on she had better do her paddling in private. It would never do if the tale went round that the new physio had been seen playing in the sea like a bairn. Dr McEwan would be quite sure then that all his doubts were justified.

Dr McEwan—the only partner whose wife had not been there last night. Presumably he had one; being so keen on married colleagues, he could hardly exempt himself!

Robin ate her lunch beside ruined Dunleathann Castle which sat on a low green peninsula, jutting out into the western sea. Like the southern beaches, this was another spot where she had spent many happy holiday hours. It was very warm here out of the wind, and the constant hum of bees in the purple rhododendrons all around was very soothing. The western air was so relaxing that after a while Robin found she could hardly keep awake. But duty called. Having made a promise which common sense required her to keep, reluctantly she tidied up the remains of her lunch and ambled back to the car.

The tiny village of Dunleathann was due west of Bratanport and a rocky, precipitous road through the mountains connected them. It was only a few miles across the island, and much longer either way round the coast, but Robin hadn't got a spare tyre until that puncture was mended, and she could just imagine Dr McEwan's comments if she got herself stranded in the wilds. So she completed her circuit of the island without stopping again and reached the Health Centre by the middle of the afternoon.

An hour or so of hard work and Robin could look round her department with pride. Now that everything was unpacked and arranged, yesterday's favourable impression was confirmed. She was just about to sort out the books and journals she had brought from London when she heard the urgent ringing of the doorbell. One of the doctors has forgotten his keys, she surmised as she sped to the entrance, but it was a middle-aged man in a clerical collar who was peering anxiously through the plateglass door.

'An accident,' he said as soon as she opened up. 'I saw the car and hoped—a doctor . . .'

'Come in and I'll phone for the one on duty. But what's the trouble, Minister? He's sure to ask.'

To her surprise he hurried back to his car without a word and lifted out a small boy, dirty, ragged, covered in blood—and still bleeding profusely from a deep gash in his leg. 'The treament-room, quickly!' commanded Robin, leading the way, with the minister explaining as they went how he had heard this crash and run out to the garden to see young Calum here sitting in the middle of his cold frame. When he had deposited the child on the treatment-room couch, Robin asked him to ring Dr Drummond from Reception while she staunched the bleeding. That done, she asked her patient how he had managed to fall into the cold frame. 'And just you leave that leg propped up the way I put it,' she added when he looked like climbing down. 'We don't want it to start bleeding again, do we?'

'Wummen!' growled the child under his breath. 'I wus on'y sittin' on the wa'—and then I fell aff it.'

'And why were you sitting on the wall?' asked Robin, tongue in cheek. She knew a thing or two about small boys.

'Jest lookin. Here! Whit d'ye think ye're daein'?' he demanded fiercely when she started to unbutton his filthy shirt.

'You've made such a mess of yourself that all these will have to come off. And your shorts.'

'Ye're no' gettin' ma breeks,' he said, clutching at them with his bloodstained fingers.

'I am so. How else can I clean you up and count the damage before the doctor comes? I don't know what you were after in the minister's garden but I hope it was worth it. You look as if you'd been wrestling with a crocodile!'

'My early strawberries, and he squashed the lot when he fell on them,' explained the minister, coming back just then. 'Dr Drummond is answering a call at the south end, so his wife is contacting Dr McEwan. He should be here very soon, Nurse—er . . .'

'Robin Maxwell, the new physio,' she explained, continuing to sponge the boy's many cuts with antiseptic.

'Ah, yes. I should have guessed.' He managed to introduce himself as the Reverend Lachlan Morrison before sitting down abruptly, looking rather pale.

Robin felt sorry for him. Not everybody could take the sight of so much blood. 'I can manage fine until the doctor comes if you have to get away, Mr Morrison,' she offered tactfully. 'Besides, there's blood on your suit and it really ought to be cleaned off as soon as possible.'

He was obviously relieved and, saying he hoped they would meet next time in happier circumstances, he patted Calum awkwardly on the shoulder—eyes averted from the damaged leg—and took his departure.

'Och, he's no' a bad auld bugger,' observed the boy Calum before the good man was fairly through the door.

'Any more of that and I'll wash your mouth out as well,' warned Robin severely. 'That's terrible language—especially for a wee boy like you.'

'Ah'm no' wee, ah'm twelve.'

She simply couldn't believe it. He was so puny and, now that she had washed off most of the dirt, pale and undernourished looking too. When Rory McEwan arrived soon after, Calum was wolfing down the remains of Robin's lunch.

He acknowledged her briefly en route to look at the child, then, noticing the sandwich box Calum was clutching, he said grimly, 'It's to be hoped he doesn't need a general anaesthetic.'

'I thought of that before I fed him, and he doesn't.'

'You seem very sure about that.'

'Well, yes, I am. There are no bones broken and all his cuts are superficial except for that nasty gash on his left calf.'

He examined that first, then said to the boy, 'You've fairly done it this time, ye wee divil.' Grudgingly he added, 'And you've done very well here, Miss Maxwell.'

Robin hardly had time to register the unexpected praise, though, before he was asking her why she hadn't dressed the little cuts.

Robin drew in her breath on a hiss. What a man! 'I would have—but for the fact that he cut himself on glass. I thought you would want to look at them first.'

'That's right.' The so-and-so—he'd been trying to catch her out. 'As I said before, Miss Maxwell, you've done very well here. Well beyond the call of duty—for a physio.'

She shrugged. 'Not really. It was just a matter of common sense.'

'Which is a very rare commodity, so prize it.' He continued to probe and search for splinters of glass embedded in Calum without finding any. At last he straightened up. 'Right. We'll see to the smallest cuts first and then you can help me stitch up this leg.' He went over to the drugs cupboard for some local anaesthetic, saying over his shoulder, 'You'll need to have a couple of jags, Calum. Usual rates?'

'Aye—I guess so. I dinnae like the needle, ken,' he explained to Robin. 'So Dr Rory always gi'es us a pund if I dinnae greet.'

'From which I gather that you're a regular customer here,' she returned with a smile.

'Aye, ain o' the best. Dr Rory says he'll no' be oot o' work whiles Ah'm aboot.'

'That's for sure,' confirmed Calum's hero in a tone of

resignation. The anaesthetic injected without protest, he said, 'That'll take a while to work, so finish your banquet—it'll take your mind off what we're doing to the rest of you.' He drew Robin over to the sink so that they could scrub up. 'Do you know what happened to him this time?' he asked. Robin told him what the minister had told her. 'Lucky you were here,' he considered. 'That child can't afford to lose too much blood. He's anaemic already.'

'I'm not surprised. He's obviously not getting enough to eat. How come——?'

He stopped her with a warning gesture. 'Now, now—I'll tell you all about him some other time.'

The child maintained a stolid silence throughout the lengthy business of dressings, and even lengthier stitching, but as soon as he was patched up he demanded, 'Do I get ma pund now, Dr Rory?'

'I should think you might,' agreed Rory McEwan with suppressed amusement, paying up.

'And now can Ah go?'

'No you cannot. You're getting a shot of something to stop that leg getting infected and then it's the hospital for you until it heals, m'lad.'

'Honest?' Calum was as pleased as if he was being sent to a five-star hotel.

'Honest.' In an aside to Robin he said quietly, 'If I let him home in this state he'd have a generalised septicaemia in no time. That family's not overly fond of soap and water.' Then he actually gave her a full-scale smile as he asked whether she would mind staying with the boy while he went home for his car. 'I was at a friend's house when the call came through and she dropped me off. It was quicker.'

She, registered Robin as she answered, 'Yes, of course I'll stay with him.'

'Can we no' go in hers?' asked Calum beguilingly. 'Ah've niver been in one of they wee Japs.'

'Certainly not,' said Dr McEwan with a ferocious scowl. 'Miss Maxwell has got quite enough to do here without ferrying you about.'

'Well then, can you no' drive her caur, Doctor?' He bent lambent eyes on Robin that would have melted granite. 'You wouldnae mind, would ye, miss? It'd be sich a treat—and me hurt that bad.'

She simply couldn't help laughing at him. 'All right— I'll give Doctor the keys, but I'm warning you it's not exactly a Rolls-Royce.'

'You don't have to . . .' began Rory as she took the keys out of her pocket and handed them over.

'It's all right. I don't mind—it'll be quicker for you and, as you pointed out, I've still got things to do here.'

'Ye're awfie kind, miss,' considered Calum. 'Is she no', Doctor?' But Doctor, it seemed, hadn't yet formed an opinion about that.

By the time she heard Rory McEwan returning, Robin had arranged most of her books; the rest would have to wait until she could acquire another shelf. He came to return her car keys and to her amazement he was also carrying a mug of tea in each hand. 'Just thought you might be ready for this—I know I am,' he said carelessly, putting her tea on the desk and wandering over to inspect her library. 'This is some collection you've got here,' he discovered.

'I stocked up before I came, knowing I couldn't go running to a hospital library every time I wanted to check a point.'

'But that lot must have cost you a month's salary.'

'Not really—I've had some of them for ages. Anyway, I happen to think it's worth it.'

Thoughtfully he stroked his formidable chin with a well-shaped tanned hand. 'Perhaps we could make you a contribution from the annual budget,' he said, amazing her again. 'Talking of which, you must let me know if there is anything else you would like for your department.'

'Except for another shelf or two, I can't think of anything. Somebody has put a lot of thought into equipping this place. That would be my predecessor, I suppose.'

'Correct.'

'Strange,' she said slowly. 'I mean, to go to so much trouble and then leave before it was ready. Was she ill?'

'No,' he answered shortly. 'She just found that life in Vallersay didn't suit her, that's all. But I'm afraid I'm detaining you needlessly, Miss Maxwell. You must be anxious to get away now that you've done what you came for.' His tone was cool, the beginnings of comradeship gone, and he was so obviously determined to be rid of her that Robin had no choice but to agree.

'Er—yes. Well, I will be going then, Dr McEwan.'

'That's right—and thanks very much for your help.'

'It was nothing,' Robin answered quietly as she gathered up her things and left the room. She simply didn't understand it. He had seemed to be thawing out nicely and then suddenly—for no reason that she could see—he had clammed up again. Practically thrown her out, in fact, and before she could drink the tea that had been his own idea. Just doesn't believe in getting too friendly with the hired help, she supposed, as she drove away. Fortunately that didn't seem to be the case with the other doctors and their wives, or she might have been in for rather a lonely time here.

Robin reached Black Rock with just enough time for a shower and a change of clothes before dinner. This being their first glimpse of her, her entry into the dining-room brought her curious glances from the other guests. Over coffee in the lounge afterwards, Robin was buttonholed by an effusive over-dressed lady of uncertain age who said she was sure that Miss Maxwell, being a physiotherapist, would be fascinated to hear all the things that had gone wrong with her latest operation. Robin bore about half an hour of that before saying desperately that she was very sorry but she simply had to make a phone call. She gave some carefully edited first impressions to her parents who were delighted to hear from her so soon. Then, wary of a second encounter with the voluble Mrs Ferguson, she ran upstairs for a jacket and sauntered out into the cool evening.

Practically everybody else in Bratanport had had the same idea and the shore-side road was thronged. Robin walked as far as the huddle of old buildings at the pierhead, then down the pier to the far end where the ferry came in. She studied the moon's round reflection, floating lazily in the calm waters of the bay, as her mind skimmed over the events of the day, sticking inevitably at the strange abruptness of Dr McEwan's reversal into cool reserve. Getting on the right side of him would take some doing. But why?

She became aware of a cold wet nose nuzzling her hand and looked down to see a beautiful golden retriever gazing up at her. She bent and fondled its ears, getting exuberant licks and whimpers in return. 'Well, thank you very much, you lovely thing,' she said. 'Thank heaven not all the natives are hostile.'

A man's firm step approached and then Robin jumped as Rory McEwan said, 'That sounds as if you'd had an unfortunate experience.'

'Er—oh,' she said stupidly, wondering how to explain her remark truthfully without giving offence. The dog went on licking her hand and she fondled it again to give herself time.

Rory bent down and snapped a leash on its collar, demonstrating ownership. 'I don't understand this, she doesn't bother with women as a rule.' Apparently the dog's behaviour had diverted him. 'We were down on the beach when she suddenly took off like a rocket and belted up the steps on to the pier. Did you call her?'

'I didn't even see her until she was right beside me. Anyway, I don't know her name. What is it?'

'Eorna. It means barley, which is just about her colour.'

'Eorna,' murmured Robin thoughtfully, sending the animal into raptures again. Rory repeated that he simply couldn't understand it. Robin thought he sounded quite put out.

'I've always got on well with dogs and children,' she told him, stooping to give Eorna another pat. 'At least you know where you are with them.'

'That sounds rather cryptic,' he considered.

'It wasn't meant to.' But wasn't it just? 'And talking of children, you promised to tell me about Calum some time. Unless of course you're in a hurry.'

'Not at the moment, so if you're really interested, here's the story. Calum's mother is one of an island tinker family who went away to Glasgow and got herself into trouble, as they like to say here. She may or may not have married Calum's father, but she left him last year and brought the boy back here. They're squatting with the rest of the clan in a ruined cottage up on the moors and the boy runs wild.'

'Can nothing be done? He seems rather a bright child. A care order perhaps?'

'We thought of that, but he isn't ill-treated.'

'But he's not fed properly, I'm certain.'

'You're probably right, but you can't take a child into care because nobody in the family can cook. And his small size could well be genetic. I don't know his father but his

mother is tiny and . . .' His voice was drowned out by the
roar of engines as a pack of teenage motorcyclists swept
down the pier.

With tremendous presence of mind, Rory shoved Robin
and the dog into a narrow cleft between a lorry and a great
pile of fish boxes. If he hadn't, they would have been
flattened for sure.

The pack wheeled round and rode off, the din dying
away as suddenly as it had come. 'Are you all right?' Rory
asked Robin, having first comforted his dog.

'Y-yes, I'm fine,' Robin breathed unsteadily.

'You don't sound it. Are you sure you weren't
touched?'

Only by him. There was hardly any room in their refuge
and it was the unexpected contact with his hard masculine
body that had set her pulses racing—nothing else. 'No,
you were too quick for them. I'm very surprised that
Vallersay attracts morons like that, though,' she went on,
striving for normality as they stepped out onto the open
quay again.

'I didn't get a proper look at them, but I wouldn't be
surprised if they were locals. A bunch of them hangs about
the Italian ice-cream place, when they're not riding the
range like that.' He bent down and fondled Eorna. 'Come
on, my beauty, we'd better see your new friend home. We
can't have her getting mown down before we've got any
work out of her, can we?'

'You don't have to bother. I think they went the other
way,' said Robin quickly.

'Could be, but we're only out for a walk, so it makes no
difference which way we go.' He put out his free hand and
rubbed at something on the shoulder of her jacket. Robin
flinched at the contact, which was nearly as upsetting as
before. 'Sorry about that,' he said, meaning the stain. 'I'm
afraid it's grease off the lorry. I hope your coat isn't

ruined.'

'I sh-shouldn't think so. And but for your prompt action I'd be on my way to join Calum in the hospital by now.'

Mentioning the boy again had been fortunate. Rory talked about him nearly all the way back to Black Rock, leaving Robin free to worry about the extraordinary effect he seemed to be having on her. She wasn't usually this susceptible—especially not to men she knew nothing about, and didn't even like. But then she wasn't usually as unhappy and neglected as she had been of late. Over-reaction due to deprivation, she diagnosed as they reached the gates of the guest house. 'Thank you very much for seeing me home, Doctor,' she said formally to counter-balance her recent strange reactions. Then she bent down to the dog. 'And you too, you lovely thing.'

'No bother,' was Rory's casual answer. 'Eorna wouldn't have had it any other way, would you, *caileag*? See you tomorrow.' He hauled his reluctant pet down on to the beach and, at a safe distance from the new attraction, he let her off the leash. Robin watched them out of sight before turning and walking up to the house.

CHAPTER THREE

ROBIN was up with the lark next morning—or, more precisely, with a flock of quarrelling gulls. No way was she going to be late for work on her first day. She left her car at the garage to have that puncture fixed and walked the rest of the way, arriving with ample time to spare. Even so, Rory McEwan was there before her as Morag McPhail, the pretty young receptionist, explained. 'Doctor has several important phone calls to make before surgery,' she added, leaving Robin to wonder how and when she was supposed to report.

Dr McLeod resolved that one for her when he came to Reception moments later to collect his morning list. 'Not to worry, my dear,' he said when she had explained her problem. 'Rory and I have things to discuss before surgery, so I'll let him know you're here.'

'Thank you very much,' she answered fervently, surprised to find how relieved she felt. She hadn't realised that yesterday afternoon's snub and that extraordinary encounter on the pier had affected her so much.

Apart from the fact that all her patients showed a lively curiosity about her, which hampered her attempts to find out what she needed to about them, Robin had no fault to find with the first part of her morning. She was just writing up her fifth treatment record when Rory McEwan appeared in the doorway. Today, officially on duty, he wore a dark suit and an air of quiet authority. 'Good morning, Dr McEwan,' said Robin, scrambling quickly to her feet.

'Ah—so you are here,' he observed without so much as a good morning in return.

Dr McLeod must have forgotten then—or else miscalculated—but hiding behind him wouldn't, she suspected, go down very well with a man like this. 'When I got in at half eight, I was told you were busy so—so I was waiting to be sent for at your convenience,' she explained meekly, with what she hoped was the right expression to match.

'Were you, now? I hadn't thought of that.'

Difficult to tell whether that slight twitch of his well-cut mouth was amusement or not. 'I'm sorry if I got it wrong,' she offered.

He shrugged that off. 'I'd better see your documents—just in case you're an impostor.'

'No such luck, I'm afraid.'

Robin had hoped to raise a positive smile with that, but he merely answered laconically, 'Too bad.'

She made a mental note not to try out any more jokes on him until the climate picked up, as she unlocked her desk and took out her diplomas, letter of appointment and P45.

After scrutinising them carefully he said, 'Everything seems to be in order, but see my secretary later on, will you? She has some forms for you to sign. Any problems?' he felt constrained to ask.

'None so far, thank you, Dr McEwan.'

'Good. I think that's all for the present, then.'

Robin watched him depart and wondered how long this to-ing and fro-ing was going to last. Cool reception on Saturday, slight thaw yesterday—thanks to her handling of Calum's accident—onset of arctic conditions almost immediately afterwards thanks to heaven only knew what; then the climate really quite pleasant last night after he had saved her from being mown down on the pier. Now she seemed to be back where she started. Of course there was always the possibility that she was reading too much into his reactions, since she seemed to be more than normally aware of him. Robin thrust that idea angrily aside as being too uncomfortable to contemplate. She hadn't come from the St Crispin frying pan in order to leap into the Vallersay fire!

A bell rang, signalling the end of Mrs Campbell's diathermy treatment, and Robin went to switch off the machine. 'I haird you talking to our Dr Rory,' revealed the patient as she reached for her clothes. 'He's such a lovely man—just like his blessed father before him.' She fixed Robin with a gimlet eye. 'I hope *you'll* be treating him right,' she said severely.

Robin blinked her astonishment. What on earth was the woman getting at? And what a nerve! She really couldn't let her off with that. 'I'll be very sorry if I give any of my colleagues cause for complaint,' she returned quietly. 'Now please excuse me, Mrs Campbell. I think I heard my next patient coming in.'

With Mrs Campbell's departure, calm settled on the little department again and by the time Jock Anderson looked in on her just before lunchtime, Robin had forgotten that puzzling remark.

'I hope we didn't exhaust you entirely on Saturday,' he said, perching casually on the corner of Robin's desk. 'We just wanted to make you feel welcome, and never thought of your having had such a terrible time getting here.'

'I thoroughly enjoyed the evening,' Robin assured him warmly. 'Coming over on the boat, I suddenly got doubtful, and finding Lindsay's kind note waiting for me at Black Rock was exactly what I needed.'

'Great. So how was your first morning?'

'All right, I think. At least I haven't killed anybody yet.'

'Give it time,' he quipped as Morag came in to tell him

he was wanted on the phone.

'Coming, lassie.' He turned back to Robin. 'Two things. First, could you look at your schedule and see if you can find time for an ante-natal class—I've got four likely lassies for you—and secondly, a message from Lindsay. She wondered if you'd like to have supper with her on Thursday—just the two of you. That's the night she lets me out to golf with the lads.'

'I'd love that,' Robin accepted eagerly. 'And of course I'll fit in that class.'

'Good lass. I can see you're going to be a real asset,' he said approvingly. 'Well, I'd better away now. Be seeing you.'

Robin hummed to herself as she tidied up her department prior to going for lunch. Jock's friendly manner, their brief exchange, and Lindsay's invitation had quite cancelled out the hiccups of the morning.

Presumably there would be somebody in the building during the lunch hour, if only to man the phone, but, knowing herself to be on probation with the boss, Robin took the precaution of locking her treatment-room before crossing the road and going down on the fore-shore to eat Mrs McKenzie's idea of a snack. Used to a hurried sandwich in the crowded canteen at St Crispin's, she found it heaven to sit there in air that was cool and pure with the sea practically at her feet and real mountains—not a travel poster—to look at.

'Mind if I join you?' asked a girl's soft voice, and Robin turned to see Morag standing beside her.

She patted the rock she was sitting on. 'Please—I'd welcome some company.'

'Would you be feeling homesick then?' asked Morag sympathetically.

'Not really—just very much the new girl.'

'You'll soon settle down, with the doctors all so lovely

to work for. I ought to know—I've been with the practice since I left school. I started in old Dr McEwan's time.'

'He'll be retired now,' supposed Robin.

'No, he died just over a year past,' returned Morag sadly. 'That was when Dr Rory came home to take over. They say if he'd stayed in Glasgow he would have ended up a top surgeon for sure—he had a fine post with a professor, no less—yet home he came. He'd promised, you see.'

That must have been the sacrifice Miss Crombie had mentioned, and Robin realised she'd been quite wrong to suppose he was only in Vallersay because he hadn't made the grade in hospital. She was surprised to discover she was feeling slightly ashamed.

Morag chattered on at length about the practice and the patients without revealing anything more about Rory McEwan. In the end, Robin had to interrupt her, being due at the hospital. 'We must lunch together again though,' she suggested.

'I'd like that fine.' Morag looked suddenly roguish. 'I should be going too—it's my turn for the switchboard— but och, another five minutes will not matter, I'm thinking.'

Robin smiled at this example of island *manana*. 'I'd like to stay too, but unfortunately there's only one of me. 'Bye, Morag.'

Just as on Saturday, Miss Crombie was on the look-out. She introduced Robin to Sister Urquhart who had been off duty over the weekend, then invited her to come to her office later on and tell how her first day had gone.

'It's great to get a physio at last,' said Sister as Matron bustled off, 'but I'm afraid you're going to find working here very different from what you're used to.'

'That's exactly what I'm hoping. I'm tired of all the stress and drama of a big hospital.' Whether he believed

her or not, Robin intended to stick with the reason she had
given Rory McEwan.

Sister said she knew exactly what Robin meant. 'I felt
the same myself when I came to work here ten years ago
and I've never regretted it.' She was wearing a wedding-
ring, noticed Robin, so presumably was approved of by
the doctor-in-charge. 'I know Dr Rory showed you all the
patients on Saturday,' Sister continued, startling Robin
who thought she was having her mind read again. 'So I'll
leave you to it, but if there's anything you need, I'll not be
far away.'

Robin thanked her, then skimmed quickly through her
referral cards. Used as she was to working on one
specialised unit at a time, the variety she had here
suggested she'd need to cultivate the mental agility of a
grasshopper. She counted several chests, a stroke, some
orthopaedics, a couple of post-ops and even two post-
natals for good measure.

Ladies first, she decided, starting with the little soul
Rory McEwan had obliged her to treat on Saturday. She
was now obviously over the crisis that had brought her
into hospital, but two other chest cases were not and
Robin decided to discuss them with Matron.

Having completed her ward work, she was just leaving
the men's ward when she was hailed by an indignant
Calum. 'You werena' gaein' tae speak tae us,' he accused.

Robin checked and hurried over to him. 'I did look for
you when I came into the ward, but you weren't here,' she
apologised.

'Naw, weel . . .' A dusky flush spread over his thin
cheeks. 'I wuss awa' tae—tae the toilet. Some wee lassie
took us in a wheelchair and I telt her I could a' walked.
An' she stopped outside the door a' the time! It's nae
decent,' he burst out, 'and I dinnae like it here near as
much as I thocht I would.'

'Never mind. You won't be here long if you're good,'

soothed Robin. Sitting down on his bed she continued earnestly, 'If you walk on that leg too soon it'll take much longer to heal—that's why nurse took you in a chair. And she waited for you in case you needed help, because you mustn't stand on it either. Dr McEwan will tell you when it's all right to walk, so will you promise me . . .'

'Ach, ye're a' on the same side!' Calum wasn't one to prolong an argument he didn't look like winning. 'Whit aboot ma claes now? Whit did ye dae wi' 'em?'

'They're in an awful mess, but I'll have them ready by the time you're allowed to dress.' Robin took a large bar of chocolate out of her tunic pocket and Calum's eyes gleamed at sight of it. 'See? I didn't forget you,' she said, 'but first you've got to promise not to get out of bed unless nurse says you may.'

'Aye, awricht.' It was worth agreeing to get his hands on that chocolate. But, 'Wummen!' he growled defiantly once it was his.

As she left the ward, Robin was chuckling at his bid for independence, but her face was serious by the time she knocked on Matron's door. 'You're looking gey thoughtful, lassie,' said that lady when she opened it.

Robin took the offered chair. 'I've got a bit of a problem,' she said. 'Most of my patients can wait till afternoon for treatment, but a couple of the chests should have been seen first thing as well. Would the walls of Jericho fall down if I asked to change things round a bit?'

'Not as far as I'm concerned,' returned Matron. 'Why don't you talk to the doctors about it?'

'Yes, I will. How do you think they'll react?' She meant one doctor in particular.

'I'd have thought you were the one to decide your priorities, but talk to them—it can do no harm,' argued Matron. 'Dr McEwan will be here in a minute to look at his patients, so you can discuss it with him over a nice cup of tea.'

Robin very nearly said that in her short experience, Dr McEwan definitely wasn't at his best over a nice cup of tea, but just in time she substituted, 'I wouldn't want him to think I was out to change everything the minute I arrived, so perhaps I'll wait and get my ideas down on paper the way we were told to at St Crispin's.'

She hadn't heard Rory McEwan come in and jumped to her feet like a scalded cat when he asked in a tone of gentle patience, 'And what is it you were told to do at St Crispin's, Miss Maxwell?'

'N-nothing important, Dr McEwan,' she muttered. She wanted to think this thing through and ask a few questions of the other doctors before putting forward a revised timetable.

'Now that I cannot believe. Surely everything going on at St Crispin's is of the utmost importance.'

'I was only telling Miss Crombie that if—if we wanted to make any changes, we were told to write out our ideas for discussion.'

'That sounds very sensible.' He accepted a cup of tea from Matron with the sudden brief smile that could transform his face, but it faded as he turned to ask Robin what it was she wanted to change. 'And please sit down again,' he directed. 'Then I can too.'

Robin did as she was told. 'I'm just a bit—anxious about how best to fit in ward patients who need more than one treatment a day.' In for a penny, in for a pound. 'Would it be all right if I postponed morning outpatients until I'd been to see the chests here?'

'I see your problem,' he agreed, 'but there is the other side of things in a rural community like ours, with a poor bus service. At a guess I'd say your first patients live out in the wilds and asked for early appointments so as to get lifts with somebody who works in Bratanport.'

'I'm sorry—I hadn't thought of that.'

'You don't have to be sorry—you're quite right. There is a clash of priorities which you cannot be expected to appreciate on your first day.' Rightly or wrongly, Robin felt she was being reproved. 'However, when you're more familiar with all the various calls on your time, I'm sure you'll work something out.'

'Thank you, Doctor—I shall certainly try,' she returned, outwardly quiet and inwardly seething. Would she never get it right? She turned to Miss Crombie. 'Meanwhile, would you mind if I come in at eight tomorrow morning to treat those patients, Matron?'

'Well no, dear, but isn't that rather unfair on you?'

'Perhaps Miss Maxwell is thinking of finishing earlier,' suggested Dr McEwan. 'I suppose that might be a solution.' He didn't sound too sure of it.

'I can't be certain about that until I find out if my last outpatients of the day are from out of town and will be getting lifts home,' said Robin, turning his argument against him, but in a very respectful tone. 'As far as I'm concerned, I only want to do what is best for all my patients.' Even if you don't believe me, she wanted to add. She replaced her cup on the tea-tray and stood up. 'Thanks very much for the tea, Miss Crombie—and for being so understanding.'

Robin was nearly sure that Rory McEwan swore under his breath as she left the room because of the way Miss Crombie said so quickly, 'Don't be hard on her, Rory. I think she'll do very well. She cares.' But what he said in reply Robin wasn't destined to know because the spring-loaded door clicked shut behind her.

Dr Drummond was leaving too, and they walked back to the Centre together. He was obviously wearing his anaesthetist's hat because he said, 'Y'know, young Robin, one or two of our chests up there could do with treatment more than once a day.'

'I noticed,' she said, 'so tomorrow I'm going to see them before I start at the Centre.'

'Good lass,' he said, giving her shoulder an approving pat. 'I knew they'd sent us a winner this time.'

They continued to exchange ideas and found themselves in total agreement, but when they went to their own rooms—Archie had a surgery to take—Robin's mind whipped back to that earlier comment of his. A winner this time, he had said. Not only had her predecessor not taken to life in Vallersay, but it sounded as if she'd not been quite up to the job either. Well, it was always easier to follow a bad act than a good one, she reflected hopefully as she went to treat her last patients of the day.

Work all done, Robin dashed along to the garage to get her car before it closed. It was standing in the forecourt, waiting for her. 'One new tyre and one puncture repaired as directed,' said the cheerful proprietor, going on to name a charge no higher than she would have paid in London. Robin thanked him and was assured it was always a pleasure to be of service to Dr Rory and his team.

That man has got the whole island bewitched, she was thinking as she left the office and, being so preoccupied, she almost collided with a man who was crossing the forecourt. He steadied her with hands on her shoulders, then let out a long, low whistle. 'Little Robin Maxwell—it just has to be. I'd know that remarkable hair of yours anywhere, even after all this time.'

She looked up at him. Long, tousled hair streaked prematurely grey, riotous beard, steel-rimmed specs and clothes not more than three stages superior to Calum's. 'I'm sorry, I don't think . . .' she stammered.

He let her go with a twisted grin. 'I'm not surprised you don't recognise me. My folks don't either—or rather they don't choose to. I'm Dougal McKnight.'

The son of her father's old friend and colleague! Robin stared, trying in vain to find some resemblance to the earnest, gangling boy who had shared so many of her childhood escapades. 'There's a bar next door,' he said, taking her by the elbow and steering her towards it. 'We may as well do our catching up in there.'

The place was crowded and none too clean. It smelled strongly of smoke and spilled beer. Also, Robin seemed to be the only woman in the place, but Dougal seemed quite at home there, even to the extent of having his own corner seat. 'So you finally got your way and became a painter, then,' Robin observed some time later when Dougal had brought her up to date.

He lit his fifth cigarette as if he really needed it and between puffs he agreed. 'And for all the good it's done me so far, I might as well have followed Father into the bank.' He shrugged. 'But there, the art world was always slow to recognise genius. Meantime, I just about keep body and soul together churning out western sunsets for the tourists.' Dougal's eyes roamed thoughtfully over Robin's clear-skinned oval face and bright curls. 'I'd like you to sit for me some time,' he decided, 'but now it's your turn for the inquisition, lassie. What in all the world brought you back to Vallersay?'

Robin told him what she'd tried to make Rory McEwan believe, and Dougal accepted it, which was both restful and comforting. Despite their dingy surroundings, she stayed there talking to him until it was time to hurry along to Black Rock for dinner.

It wasn't until she was about to enter the lounge for coffee after the meal that she remembered Calum's clothes. If tomorrow turned out anything like today, she'd have no time to deal with them then. Besides, Mrs Ferguson was bearing down on her fast and going now would spare her another chapter of an amazing medical history. 'Work calls, I'm afraid,' said Robin to that disappointed lady as she headed for her car. It was raining and not at all the evening for walking.

The briefest inspection was enough for Robin to decide to throw out most of Calum's things and buy him new ones. She had just washed his T-shirt and jersey and was hanging them up to dry on a line she'd noticed in the boiler-room when she heard footsteps she was beginning to recognise coming purposefully down the corridor. She turned defensively as Rory McEwan appeared in the doorway.

His gaze flickered over the washing before landing speculatively on Robin's face. 'I thought that was your car outside. Are those Calum's things?' She nodded. 'There's no need to go over the top, you know—you've made a wonderful impression on nearly everybody already.'

'Except you.' It was out before she had time to consider the wisdom of it.

'I prefer to reserve judgement,' he returned coolly.

Robin sighed. 'I'm not out to impress—and how was I to know there'd be anybody about to be impressed at this time of the evening? I promised him—and one doesn't break promises to a child.'

'Or to adults either, I should hope.'

'Areed.' She turned away and took the garments off the line.

'Now what are you doing?' he wanted to know.

'I'll dry them at the boarding house as you seem rather displeased.'

'You told me you had no friends here,' he said abruptly, apparently with total irrelevance.

'Which was quite true. At least . . .' she hesitated. But she hadn't known about Dougal then.

'Hah!' he snapped as if he'd caught her out in the most tremendous lie.

Robin gazed up at him in astonishment. 'It's clear that I've angered you in some way, Dr McEwan, and I wish you would tell me how. Otherwise I may not be able to avoid doing it again.'

'Dougal McKnight,' he said as if that explained everything.

It didn't. The Vallersay telegraph was obviously functioning at breakneck speed if he'd already heard about that meeting, but what was so wrong about it?

'What about him?' she asked with genuine wide-eyed innocence.

Rory took a deep breath. 'I'm not blaming you,' he said. 'You've only just come and are not familiar with our ways. Even so, I'd have thought you'd know better than to spend hours drinking in a place like that wretched bar with a man you'd only just picked up in the street—and such a man too. This isn't London, you know. As a professional in a little place like this, you have a certain position to maintain if you want the respect of the community.'

She had to hand it to him: not many people could have crammed that many insults into one short speech. 'I didn't know that renewing acquaintance with a childhood friend could prejudice my position,' she returned deliberately. 'And just because Dougal isn't very successful in his chosen profession, there's no reason to look down on him. As for the rest,' he looked like cutting in so she raised her voice. 'As for the rest, it's a pity your spies didn't tell you I was drinking tonic water because I can't take alcohol. But then that might have spoiled the story. I do agree with you about the bar, though. It's an awful place and I shan't be going there again.'

'Well that is something, I suppose.' He swallowed hard. 'Look, I'm not trying to dictate the pattern of your life here—just pointing out the pitfalls of living in such a tight-knit community. Everything you do will come under scrutiny—so choose your friends with care. That's all.'

'I'll remember,' she said for form's sake. 'But I'll need a better reason than fear of public opinion to turn my back on an old friend who went out of his way to make me feel welcome.' Unlike you, hung upspoken in the air between them.

'How was I to know you already knew the man when you'd told me you had no friends here?' he asked gruffly. 'And for heaven's sake put Calum's stuff back on the line. You're ruining that nice dress.' He stamped out and away down the corridor, leaving Robin to wonder who had won that particular bout. Honours even, perhaps?

CHAPTER FOUR

'AND iss this not a nice surprise?' asked Mrs Mary McKenzie-Bratanport Bakers and infected bunions—when Robin walked into the ward.

'Yes indeed. We were only just saying that, being Saturday, we would not be seeing Miss Maxwell the day,' seconded her cousin-in-law Mrs Agnes McKenzie—Iolair Tearoom and gastric ulcer.

'I haven't come to bully everybody,' laughed Robin, 'but I think that Mrs MacLean might need a bit of encouragement with her breathing exercises.'

'Aye, aye, the puir soul. A very uncomfortable business it is getting the gall bladder out, and her with the bronchitis since we were all at the school,' was the contribution of Miss Jean McKenzie—dressmaker and diverticulitis—busy even now stitching a new zip into Sister Urquhart's good tweed skirt.

'I'll not say I'm that pleased to see you myself,' admitted the patient Robin had come to see. 'But I know fine it iss for my own good.'

'I hope your breathing is easier for getting all that nasty stuff off your chest,' said Robin when she was settling Mrs MacLean comfortably again after a successful treatment.

'I'll not deny it, but I'll be gey glad when this stops hurting.' She stroked her operation wound tenderly.

'Give it another twenty-four hours and you'll not know yourself,' promised Robin. 'Meanwhile, keep up the deep breathing and I'll be back to see you later on.'

Except for emergencies, Robin was officially off duty

57

at weekends but, as she was there anyway, she decided to spend some time with Mr Sinclair, the new stroke patient, after she had exchanged cheerful goodbyes with the women. Part of his trouble was his temporary loss of speech, but he expressed his gratitude by pressing Robin to take a bar of chocolate.

All my patients such a pleasure and only the boss a pain in the neck, she thought as she left the men's ward to another cheerful chorus of farewells. She had been in Vallersay for six weeks now, hadn't put a foot wrong and enjoyed the trust and good will of all her colleagues but Rory McEwan, who still treated her with formal reserve. It was really rather unnerving. 'If he keeps it up I could easily go and do something awful out of sheer nerves,' she muttered grimly as she opened the front door.

Her mood lightened the minute she stepped outside. Who could possibly feel depressed when looking at this splendid panorama of mountain, moor and sea? After watching the ferry leave the pier and head seawards through all the pleasure boats riding at anchor, Robin was just about to tear herself away from the view when Sister Urquhart came panting up behind her. 'Thank goodness I caught you, Robin. Old Mrs Jane McKenzie has just broken her Zimmer,' she announced.

'How on earth did she manage that?' wondered Robin.

'You may well ask, *mo ghaoil*, but she has and it was the last one we had. Do you have one to spare down yonder?'

Robin said yes, of course she had, and promptly offered to go and get it.

'I knew I could count on you,' said Sister, going back inside to pacify the patient while Robin hurried off down the rhododendron path Rory McEwan had introduced her to on her first day.

His Range Rover stood in the car park at the Centre

even though this was his weekend off. Typical, she thought, as she paused to exchange affectionate greetings with Eorna through the open window. Whatever she might think of him as a man, as a doctor he now had her whole-hearted approval. Even at St Crispin's she hadn't come across anybody more competent and hardworking. And having to admit that made it all the more difficult to put up with his attitude towards her. Even if he never thawed out she would have to stay at least a year if she was to get a decent reference. She felt reasonably sure that any of the other doctors would give her a glowing testimonial, but then the first question put to her at interview would be—why didn't you ask the senior M.O.? 'You've gone and got yourself into a bit of a hole, *caileag*,' she muttered as she pushed open the heavy main door.

Bulky things like walking aids were kept in a store next to the treatment-room. Glancing in in passing, Robin noticed that the padlock on the dangerous drugs cupboard seemed to be hanging loose. She went in to check and snapped it shut, turning round to come face to face with Dr McEwan, hidden from sight until then by the open door. 'If you want something from that cupboard, I'd prefer it if you asked me first,' he said with patient reproach.

Damn the man—did he think she was after the heroin or what? 'I wouldn't dream of rifling the drugs, or any other cupboard,' she replied tightly. 'I was only securing it because it looked to me as if somebody had forgotten.'

'I opened it, and I had not forgotten.'

'All is well then—except for one thing. I don't like not being trusted, Dr McEwan. I don't like it at all. In fact, I'm beginning to think the best thing I can do is to hand in my notice!' She walked out head high and back rigid with indignation as she stamped down the corridor, but inside she was quaking. How had she come to make such a stupid remark so soon after facing the fact that a short stay would look very bad on her c.v.? What was it about him that made her over-react so? And drat it, she'd clean forgotten what she was in the Centre for at all this morning! Rather than risk another encounter while he was sure to be very angry with her, Robin completed the circuit of the building and crept into the storeroom from the opposite direction. Just as she came out again with the Zimmer, he emerged from the treatment-room.

'Sister Urquhart needs this for a patient in the hospital,' she said as soon as she found her voice. 'I'm taking it up to her now.'

'There is no need to explain. Walking aids are your responsibility—just as drugs are mine,' he returned heavily. He regarded her sombrely for a long, fraught second before adding, 'I think we had better find time on Monday for a serious talk, Miss Maxwell.' Then he went back into the treatment-room leaving her looking at the closed door with a fast-beating heart. He hadn't mentioned her outburst; hadn't needed to. Robin knew very well what had prompted him to decide on that talk. Just as well, really, she comforted herself as she trailed dejectedly back up the hill to the hospital. Things cannot go on like this.

While lunching with the Andersons—now her firm friends—Robin pushed the problem to the back of her mind, but sitting in the garden afterwards while Jock washed the car and the boys played commandos, she unburdened herself to Lindsay. 'I knew I'd blow my top sooner or later,' she said, having told of the morning's encounter. 'And now I've got the feeling I've given Dr McEwan the chance he's been looking for to get rid of me.'

Lindsay looked thunderstruck. 'You've got to be wrong about that,' she said firmly. 'What possible reason could Rory have for wanting to be rid of you? Jock says they're all delighted with the way you're shaping up.'

'Jock, Hamish and Archie may be—but Dr McEwan always treats me as if—as if I were an unexploded bomb.'

'I can't believe it!' Lindsay wasn't trying to be reassuring; she sounded genuinely puzzled. 'Rory isn't the man to strike up instant friendships, but I've never known hm to be unfair or discourteous.'

'He isn't. I didn't mean to imply that. Just—well, wary is perhaps the best description. It's as if he thinks I'm not what I seem and will break out and behave in some terrible way—and then he'll be justified in not trusting me. Yet he's so nice to everybody else. I don't understand it.'

'Neither do I, if it's as bad as you say.' She hesitated. 'Of course he has had—problems in the past. It could be something to do with that.'

'He hasn't got an exclusive on problems,' returned Robin bitterly. 'I've got a great big one myself and he is IT.'

Then Ian, Lindsay's youngest, fell off the climbing frame, and making sure he wasn't seriously hurt put everything else out of their minds.

Robin stayed to tea, helped Lindsay to bath the children and then visited the hospital to treat Mrs MacLean again as promised. But after that, walking back to Black Rock for dinner, she found herself going over it all again. Rory McEwan's constant watchfulness was setting her on edge, and taking most of the pleasure out of this job that was to have been the cure for David. Suddenly she realised that, disapproval or not, the cure was working. Trying to keep on the right side of That Man, and wondering ceaselessly about the reason for his attitude, was effectively preventing her from thinking too much about her lost love. The old counter-irritant principle, she thought wryly. Swap one pain for another, and you ease the first.

*　　*　　*

Robin didn't bother to dress up that night; a denim skirt
and cotton T-shirt were quite adequate for a drink with
Dougal, who always looked as if he got his clothes after
Oxfam had rejected them. 'Artist's licence,' he had said
carelessly that time he caught her looking sideways at his
dingy shirt.

'And here was I thinking it was paint,' she had riposted.

He had laughed, appreciating her wit, and had taken
just a little more trouble with his appearance after that.
But not a lot, and now Robin was used to his careless
appearance.

Not so her landlady, who made no bones about letting
Robin know how much she disapproved of her friendship
with Dougal—long-standing or not. Robin for her part
looked forward to the day when she could escape from
Mrs McKenzie's oppressive motherliness into a rented
cottage. That's if I last that long, she reflected
apprehensively, remembering Monday's threatened
showdown.

Robin had kept her vow to Rory about not going to the
unsavoury bar called the Fisherman again and, tonight,
she was meeting Dougal in Bratanport's second best, the
Smugglers' Inn.

'Ye're gey thochtful lookin' the night, ma lass,' he
observed humorously when they had exchanged greetings
and settled in a corner of the public bar.

Until now, Robin had told him nothing of her problem,
but having failed to make Lindsay understand that
afternoon, she was sorely tempted to try her luck with
him. She had discovered that, for all his apparent
indolence, Dougal was surprisingly shrewd.

He heard her out in a sympathetic silence and then he
said, 'But surely it's obvious.'

Robin gave a little gasp of astonishment and slumped
back in her seat. 'Not to me, it isn't. You'll have to

explain, Dougal.'

'It'll be to do with that girl Deirdre somebody—now what was her other name?' His brow cleared after a moment's corrugated thought. 'Mathieson—or was it Matthewson? Anyway, the one he was engaged to.'

So Rory McEwan had been crossed in love. Well, so had she, but she didn't go around distrusting innocent colleagues as a result. 'I still don't get it,' she admitted.

'D'you mean to say nobody's told you about her yet?' He finished his drink and ordered another, while Robin tried to be patient. 'Perhaps that's not so surprising, though. Naturally his colleagues wouldn't, for fear of hurting his feelings, and neither would the islanders. They're gey curious about each other and all the incomers, but they close ranks and keep quiet about themselves. Anyway, Rory brought her with him when he came home to take over from his father, but six months was enough to convince her she couldn't bear to live here permanently. I hear she did her damnedest to make Rory change his mind and go back to Glasgow. When he refused, she simply packed up and went home alone.'

'Just like my predecessor, then,' mused Robin.

'What d'you mean, like? She was your predecessor.'

Vividly Robin recalled that brief conversation at the Centre after Calum's accident. No wonder Rory had clammed up and practically thrown her out when she started asking awkward questions. All unknowingly, she had hit him right where it hurt most.

'D'you know, you even look rather like her, although she was actually rather beautiful,' Dougal continued with deplorable lack of tact. Robin noticed but was far too busy remembering other things to take offence. Like Mrs Campbell's cryptic remark about treating him right, and even before that what Lindsay had said that very first night. I'm not surprised, had been her prompt reply when

Robin said that Rory would have preferred a man or an older woman. Now she found herself feeling really sorry for him. It couldn't be easy, constantly running into your lost love's look-alike—even such a homely imitation as Dougal seemed to think her. And doing the same job, too . . .

'. . . let it worry you too much,' she suddenly realised Dougal was saying now. 'It's easy to see why you were such an unpleasant shock to him, but he'll come round once he realises how very different you are underneath.'

'I don't know about that,' she said doubtfully. Then, remembering all the times she had seen Rory about with a most attractive brunette, she said, 'Pining or not, he seems to be very well comforted as far as I can see.'

'You'll be referring to the laird's daughter. Yes, she knows what she's about, that one.' Dougal laughed lewdly. 'I wouldn't mind a bit of that sort of comfort myself. Rory's a very lucky lad.'

For some obscure reason, Robin found that a most depressing thought. 'Some folk drown their sorrows in drink, but Rory McEwan finds solace in women, then,' she quipped with forced gaiety.

'Me, I prefer both remedies,' said Dougal, draining his glass and ordering yet another dram. He gave Robin a wicked look. 'Are you sure you wouldn't like to move into the top flat when my tenants leave?'

'As I said the first time you suggested it, thanks for the kind thought but that's no way to improve my image with the boss—or the minister.' Anyway, she could be getting her cards on Monday.

But surely it won't come to that? hoped Robin some time later as she walked home alone. Dougal never came further with her than his own front door. She turned round and looked at the lights winking lazily all round the bay and realised with a jolt that she didn't want to leave

Vallersay for a long time yet. Well, tomorrow was Sunday, giving her plenty of time to come up with a convincing apology before the threatened confrontation with Rory McEwan.

As on the previous day, Robin went early to the hospital to treat her illest patients and found them all slightly improved. Then, her mind relieved on that score, she drove on to Fratini's ice-cream parlour to meet Calum.

While he was in the hospital, she had contrived to spend a few minutes with him every time she went there. The day he was discharged, she drove him home to his feckless mother, dressed in the clothes she had bought him to replace those ruined in the accident. On the way, he had solemnly adopted her as his aunt. So there was no question of forgetting all about him after that. Besides, she had grown fond of the child and enjoyed his company. The only stipulation she made was that Dr Rory wasn't to know of their friendship. He would only think she was trying to curry favour, though naturally she hadn't told Calum her reason.

Calum was late, so Robin sat down with a coffee at a table by the window and reviewed her breakfast-time conversation with Mrs KcKenzie while she waited. As usual, her landlady had asked where Robin was going. Knowing she would find out anyway, Robin had told her that she and Calum were going fishing. Mrs McKenzie had then gone on at length about the folly of letting oneself be taken advantage of by thieving wee monsters. Robin stoutly defended Calum and escaped before Dougal was dragged into the conversation, as experience had taught he surely would be.

Mrs McKenzie was getting beyond a joke and, holiday season or no, she would have to get away from Black Rock, even if she had to spend the rest of the summer in a tent!

'Whit's wrang, Robin?' asked Calum, slipping into place on the bench beside her. 'If annybody's been upsettin' ye, I'll soon sort 'em!'

Her expression changed from showers to sunshine as she signalled to the boy behind the counter to bring Calum his usual outsize sundae. 'Nothing that won't sort itself,' she assured her champion, lips twitching. 'Now tell me where we're going today. I'm dying to know.'

Only after he had downed his usual quota did Calum tell. 'It's a great wee pool and the trout as thick as corbies on a tip,' he revealed when he'd told her they'd be taking the rough mountain road that bisected the island. 'I'll tell ye whaur tae leave the caur when we come tae it. Of course if ye had a Range Rover like Dr Rory we could get nearly all the way there.'

Robin felt her lips tightening. The only flaw in their friendship was the way he would keep on mentioning his hero. 'Range Rovers cost about four times what this wee Jap, as you call it, cost me.'

'Ah'm no' knockin' it, jest tellin' ye. Onnyway, it doesnae matter aboot the walkin'. Ye're gey guid on the hills—for a wumman.'

'Thank you very much,' Robin answered meekly as she parked in the lay-by Calum had selected. 'Now what?'

'Up there,' he said, pointing to a well-used track that led through rhododendron thicket and pine forest to Ben Iolair and its satellites. 'It's jest aboot two mile, I'm thinkin'.'

Robin opened the hatch and hoisted her haversack on to her back, declining Calum's gallant offer to carry it. 'You've got the rods,' she said gravely, handing him the sticks with their string lines and hooks made out of bent pins.

'Aye, richt enough.' He shouldered them like a

seasoned angler and led the way at an amazing rate for so small a child.

When they reached the chosen spot—a quiet side-pool in an otherwise turbulent river, some way from the main track—Calum set about introducing Robin to the joys of fishing for trout. They caught nothing, but thoroughly enjoyed their morning and picnic lunch until there came a sudden violent downpour of rain.

'This wusnae forecast,' observed Calum severely with a reproving glance skywards. Then he seized Robin's hand and rushed her to the only shelter in sight—a stunted rowan tree clinging tenaciously to an overhanging rock. There they huddled together under Robin's plastic mac, waiting for the rain to cease.

After what seemed like hours, a lone hiker came swinging down the hill towards them. A large dog trotted obediently at his side until it caught a different scent, when, regardless of its master's call, it hurtled through the wet bracken, desperate to get to Robin.

'What the devil . . .?' Rory McEwan came to a halt and gazed at them in amazement, as the rain dripped steadily off his waterproof clothing.

'Me and ma auntie wuss fishing till the rain came on,' explained Calum placidly.

'You and your . . .?' Rory gave a brief shout of amusement. 'So this is why you're keeping out of trouble these days, is it?' He came and squeezed into the tiny shallow cave with them, relieving Robin of his pet, who was trying desperately to sit on her lap. 'And how long has this been going on?' he demanded.

'Aw, ages,' Calum answered for them both. 'We kinda took tae each other richt aff, did we no', Robin?'

'We certainly did,' she answered. 'Just like Eorna and me.' So that's two out of the three of you who think I'm all right, was her unspoken comment.

'On'y, you wasnae s'posed tae ken,' added Calum.

At that, Rory leaned forward far enough to peer at Robin's scarlet face half hidden under the plastic mac. 'Any particular reason for that? Apart from the fact that you've obviously been poaching today.'

'I thought we probably were,' Robin answered quickly, seizing the chance to bypass his question. 'But as we didn't catch anything, I suppose we're in the clear.'

'Deplorable,' he reckoned, though without the usual note of disapproval in his voice. 'For a moment there, I hoped you were having a beneficial effect on this keelie, but now I see it's quite the other way about.'

'Eh, watch it,' warned Calum truculently. 'She's been richt guid tae us. Who d'ye think gi'e us all ma new claes—and these?' He stuck out his spindly legs to show off new rubber boots. 'Specially fer the fishin',' he explained.

'That was very generous,' said Rory, sounding as if he really meant it. 'I hope you thanked Miss Maxwell properly.'

''Course I did! Onnyways, I take her aboot a lot an' she says it's a fair exchange, d'ye not, Robin?'

'Aye, I do,' she answered in good imitation Glasgow. 'Calum has done such a lot to help me settle down,' she added.

Rory eyed her sideways through narrowed eyes but didn't rise to that. Instead he shifted his gaze to the sky. 'In case you hadn't noticed,' he said, 'the rain is easing off, but not for long, I'm thinking. You'd be as well to make a dash for it while you have the chance.'

Calum seconded that, so they gathered up their belongings and prepared to depart. Whether or not Rory meant to go with them wasn't clear but Eorna made sure of it by dancing all round Robin.

'I simply do not understand what has come over that

animal,' said Rory, but this time he didn't sound quite so affronted.

'They say dugs aye ken,' observed Calum from his place on Robin's other side. 'Who's guid an' who isnae,' he added in case anybody hadn't got his meaning.

Robin could have kissed him. He couldn't have done better for her if she'd been coaching him for weeks. Turning round to view the effect on Rory of this bit of homely wisdom, she stumbled on a loose stone in the path. Rory stopped her falling by grabbing her roughly by the scruff of the neck. 'Kindly remember you're the only physio we've got and refrain from doing yourself an injury,' he directed as he let her go.

Robin rearranged the collar of her anorak and tried to forget the pressure of his fingers. 'Can I take it that I'm fairly useful after all then?' she asked daringly.

'Have I ever said otherwise?' asked Rory, as they gained the shelter of the forest just as the rain came on again.

It was still pelting down when they reached Robin's car and she felt bound to offer Rory a lift. He refused on the grounds that a drenched dog would make a terrible mess of the upholstery, but the minute Robin opened the door Eorna jumped in the back, regardless. 'Too late,' he said ruefully, getting in beside her and forcing her on to the floor. 'You must be thinking I've no control at all over this creature,' he said when Robin and Calum were in too.

Robin switched on the ignition and set the wipers going at maximum speed. 'I'm sure you have most of the time, Dr McEwan, but nobody's perfect. I meant Eorna, of course,' she added hastily, on meeting his quizzical look in her rear-view mirror.

'What a relief,' he returned drily.

Since that first day when she took him home from the hospital, Calum had refused to let Robin near his home, and today as usual he directed her to stop at the end of the track leading up to the neglected cottage.

To her surprise, Rory transferred to the front passenger seat when Calum got out and together they watched the boy's puny figure plodding stolidly through the rain towards his cheerless home. 'You're being extremely good to that child and he's obviously very attached to you,' he observed thoughtfully. 'But why were you so anxious that I shouldn't know about it?'

So he hadn't forgotten Calum's revelation. Robin considered a moment before answering candidly, 'I was afraid you would think I was only doing it to impress.' He wouldn't like that, but it was the truth.

'Because of what I said when I found you washing his clothes?' So he hadn't forgotten that either.

'I suppose so,' sounded less accusing than a straight-forward yes.

'But you're not,' he said positively. 'Anybody could tell that.'

'Thank you,' she muttered, feeling absurdly pleased as she set the car going again.

In silence they completed the short run to his house next door to the hospital on the hill, but when she stopped the car at his gate, Rory asked abruptly, 'Are you in a hurry?'

'No, I'm not,' she answered, taken completely by surprise.

'Good—because with Hamish McLeod off on holiday, I shall have an extra surgery tomorrow and it might be difficult to fit in that talk we agreed we needed. I suggest we have it now.'

'O-oh—all right.' Clever of him to make sure first that she wasn't pushed for time. Not so clever of her to have let the day go by without considering what she meant to say. Robin clasped her hands tightly together in her lap and waited for him to open fire.

Instead, he got out of the car and then hauled Eorna

out by her collar. 'Come on then, *caileag*,' he told Robin. 'It'll be streaming down again in a minute.' Then he set off at an easy run up the drive. Quickly Robin exchanged tramping shoes for casuals before scrambling out and running after him. She hadn't expected to be taken into the house.

In the old-fashioned kitchen, Rory kicked off his muddy boots and pulled a bath towel off the airing rack. 'I have to dry Eorna first if she's not to get a chill,' he explained. He nodded towards the kettle humming quietly to itself on top of the Aga. 'You'll find tea and a pot and cups on the dresser.'

'Right,' said Robin, beginning to feel better. Surely he wouldn't have invited her in and suggested tea if he meant to make her stick by her threat to quit. Would he?

Eorna dried and the tea made, Rory added a rich-looking fruit cake to the contents of the tea-tray. 'Grateful patient,' he explained laconically, then, telling the dog to stay put on her rug in front of the Aga and dry off, he led the way to a comfortably shabby and chintzy sitting-room and as always when in a house that fronted the bay, Robin went straight to the window and looked out. Despite the rain sluicing down the glass, she had no doubt this must be the best view she'd seen yet, and she said so.

'You really do like Vallersay, don't you?' he asked thoughtfully.

'Yes, I do,' she returned with simple sincerity.

When she turned to face him, he was watching her intently, thumbs stuck in the waistband of his jeans and grey eyes narrowed. 'Yet you're thinking of leaving.' Robin flushed slightly and looked down at her feet, saying nothing. 'The call of the town, perhaps?' he suggested.

'No! No,' she repeated more quietly. 'Nothing like that.'

'Then why?'

'I—I thought I made that clear yesterday,' she muttered.

'Sorry, I didn't quite catch that.'

I wouldn't mind betting a month's salary that you did, she thought. She took a deep breath and looked him squarely in the eye. 'May I ask a question please, Dr McEwan?'

Clearly that wasn't what he'd been expecting, but he said, 'Certainly—if it's relevant.'

'It is. Is my work satisfactory?'

'Yes, it is—so far.'

Robin decided to ignore the proviso. 'Is there anything at all you think I could do better?'

'If there were, then I'd not hesitate to say so.'

That Robin could well believe. 'So you've no complaints on that score, then. All the same, I can't help feeling that you don't—don't trust me.'

'So you said yesterday.'

This wasn't at all how she had imagined it would go. He was leaving it all to her. Did he hope then that she would say something completely outrageous and give him the excuse he needed to be rid of her? Well, she wasn't going to! 'That's why I thought about leaving,' she said carefully. 'I don't want to—I love Vallersay—but not being trusted makes me feel . . . kind of nervous. I'm not used to it.'

Rory regarded her thoughtfully, for a long fraught second, before saying quietly, 'You've spoken frankly, so I'll try to do the same.' He took another thoughtful moment before he did, though. At last, he said with obvious reluctance, 'It is my—er- unfortunate experience that city-bred girls don't take kindly to life in Vallersay, which is why I thought your appointment was so unsuitable. Couple that with a natural caution about any new and unknown member of staff and I hope you can begin to understand my doubts. All the same——' he broke off with a frown. 'I might as well tell you that our somewhat heated exchange yesterday morning left me feeling extremely annoyed, but after thinking it over, I'm bound to admit that there was some justification for your resentment. For—entirely personal reasons, I was prejudiced and I allowed that to show. I've not been fair to you and I . . .' He swallowed visibly. 'I apologise.'

It was more—much more than she would have dared to hope for, and Robin gazed up at him in astonishment. Rory shrugged ruefully. 'Your finding that so astonishing tells me a lot about your opinion of me.'

Robin felt it was her turn to be generous now. 'I don't think I've been as easy to get on with as I might have been.'

'Let's not fight for the biggest share of humble pie,' he urged with a crooked smile. 'Can I take it then that you'll not be handing in your notice?'

'Yes, you can, Dr McEwan.'

'Well, thank heaven for that. I wasn't looking forward to telling my colleagues that I'd frightened you away. They are of the unanimous opinion that the sun sets over your head.' He bent down and felt the teapot. 'Cooling fast and stewed as well, no doubt. I'll go and make some more. Make yourself at home, Robin.'

Robin! She smiled at that as she looked round the room. The furniture was good—antique and graceful—but the room needed redecorating and the faded curtains wouldn't stand another wash. It couldn't be the shabbiness of poverty; more the result of no woman in the house to notice and bother, she guessed, crossing the room to look at a large cabinet photograph of a gentle, smiling woman and a white-haired man who must once have looked much as his son did now.

The front door opening and shutting with a bang roused

Robin from this study and a moment later the sitting-room door flew open to admit the vibrant brunette she had seen so often with Rory. She was wearing an exquisitely cut peach silk shirt with matching skin-tight pants, and a priceless Paisley shawl was thrown carelessly round her shoulders. Her smile died instantly, to make way for a look of disdain, as her large brown eyes took in Robin's sensible leisure gear and her tousled curls clinging damply to her tanned forehead. 'And who are you?' she asked rudely, subtly suggesting Robin would probably feel more at home in the kitchen.

Robin's chin rose a fraction along with one winged eyebrow. 'I'm Robin Maxwell, the new physiotherapist. And you?'

The girl stared in surprise. 'Good God—I thought everybody in Vallersay knew me! I'm Selina Stuart-Strang. My father owns half the island.'

'What an awesome responsibility,' commented Robin quietly, just as Rory returned with the fresh pot of tea. He'd also brought another cup, warned by the noise Selina had made coming in.

'So sorry, darling. I seem to have burst in on some sort of professional discussion,' apologised Selena, sounding anything but sorry. 'Would you like me to go?'

He stared. 'Why on earth should I? As you see, we're just going to have tea. But you two haven't met, have you? Robin is . . .'

'Yes, I know. She told me.' Again that diminishing look for Robin and then, 'You must be very, very busy if you have to do your discussing on a Sunday.' Galling, the way she assumed that Robin couldn't possibly be paying a social call.

'Hamish went on holiday yesterday, so of course we are,' Rory answered calmly as he poured the tea.

Robin judged it tactful to go and sit at a distance on

the window-seat to drink hers, which made it a whole lot easier for Selina to try and shut her out of the conversation. But Rory kept it general. It wasn't the sort of situation to be prolonged, though, so Robin refused more tea, saying firmly that she had to be going if she was to give Mrs MacLean her second treatment before patients' supper time.

Rory saw her out, but made no reference to the conversation they were having before Selina came. Robin forgot the incident while treating her patient, but, driving back to Black Rock afterwards, she found herself wondering just how the day would have gone on if she and Rory had not been interrupted. At least they had settled their differences, though. Work would surely proceed more smoothly now.

CHAPTER FIVE

IT WAS raining steadily next morning and had been all night, judging by the size of the puddles in the flower beds all around the house. Vallersay was displaying its least attractive side. Robin shrugged philosophically, put on her waterproof and took the car to work—calling first at the hospital as usual.

Mrs MacLean's chest was quite clear now, but an old man had just been brought in from one of the remotest crofts. 'Almost certainly a fractured neck of femur,' reckoned Miss Crombie when giving Robin the news. 'So Rory will be wanting to plate it. The *bodach* is coughing away there like nothing on earth, so a spot of pre-opping won't go amiss. He hasn't the English and is nearly blind without his glasses, which nobody thought of sending with him, so good luck, Robin. Still, I'm sure you'll cope,' she added with a confident smile.

Don't bet on it, thought Robin wryly as Matron bustled off. Obviously her usual miming routine wasn't going to work this time. As luck would have it, none of the nurses on duty had the Gaelic but fortunately Mr Angus McKenzie—Bratanport hardware store and post-op double hernia—had enough to relay her instructions. It was a novel experience, involving one patient in the treatment of another, but hardly a breach of confidentiality. Everybody in the ward would have grasped what was going on anyway; in addition to his other problems, old Mr McPhail was very deaf.

This unexpected extra meant that Robin would be

lucky to get to the Centre before her first outpatient and she was dashing to the hospital when Rory McEwan came through the door. 'I can see you're in a tearing hurry,' he began, 'but if you could hang on for a few minutes I'd be obliged. I'm just going to see a new patient who'll probably be going to theatre today.'

'If it's old Mr McPhail you're meaning, then I've just spent some time with him.'

'That's him, so ten out of ten, Miss Maxwell,' he approved cheerfully before disappearing into the cloakroom to get his white coat.

Robin ran through the rain to her car. She was Miss Maxwell again this morning, whereas yesterday he had called her Robin. Ah, well, Rome wasn't built in a day, she found herself thinking as she skidded down the streaming hill to the Centre. And what precisely did I mean by that? she wondered with surprise as she parked and ran for cover.

Her first patient was the same Mrs Campbell she had crossed swords with on her first day; back for treatment to an ankle this time. She made quite a performance out of consulting her watch and the department clock as Robin panted into the treatment-room. A swift glance of her own at the clock told Robin she was exactly two minutes late. 'Good morning, Mrs Campbell,' she said firmly. 'I'm afraid I was delayed at the hospital, discussing a patient with Dr McEwan.' Rather an exaggeration, but justified. More than once, Mrs Campbell had kept her waiting much longer than that.

'I should like to try the paraffin wax,' announced the patient when Robin had gathered all the paraphernalia for giving ultrasound. 'My next-door neighbour says it's working wonders for her hands.'

'If it's Mrs Morag McKenzie you're meaning, then her problem is quite different from yours,' Robin explained patiently, 'and I can assure you this treatment is much more suitable for you. Dr McEwan thinks so too,' she added, invoking the oracle a second time.

Vanquished, Mrs Campbell bore it all in a martyred silence and merely sighed heavily when, treatment over, Robin wished her good morning and hoped she'd soon be feeling the benefit. Ah, well, there's usually one, Robin reflected philosophically, watching her patient's rigid back view disappearing. And happily next on the list was dear old Mrs McIntyre, always so cheerful in spite of being half crippled with arthritis. She had just departed after presenting Robin with a box of her famous home-made shortbread—and heaven only knew how she ever managed to make it with those hands of hers—when Archie Drummond breezed in. 'I've just seen a lady with marked osteo-arthritic changes at $C5-6$ with consequent acute pain and paraesthesiae in both arms. Can you possibly fit her in this morning for some traction and a cervical collar? She lives way up at the north end, so that'd save her one journey.'

'Sure I will, Archie. And presumably she'll need—what? Thrice weekly or daily treatment?'

• 'Whatever you think best, and thanks a million, Rob. Now I must away and get my visits done. Rory wants to operate on that hip during the lunch hour; it's the only time we can synchronise today.' He was away virtually at a run, and Robin consulted her own list which was full to bursting already.

It went on like that all morning and, lunchless except for an apple en route, Robin was thankful to escape up the hill to the hospital that afternoon. At least she knew how many cases to expect there. Putting patients two in a bed had gone out of fashion in the eighteenth century.

Her afternoon treatments completed, Robin was discussing work with Miss Crombie when a loud tummy

rumble revealed the deprived state of her digestive tract.
'Tea and scones, now,' directed Matron, shooing Robin
into her office where a loaded tray waited. 'You're just
asking for a peptic ulcer, lassie. How many times have I
told you not to skip your meals?'

The scones were light and fluffy and still warm from
the oven; Robin was on her third when Rory looked in
and was warmly invited to join the tea-party. He glanced
at Robin before saying, 'I wish I could, Ella, but
unfortunately I haven't the time. I just wanted to tell you
that I've done Mr McPhail's post-op check and all is
well, but don't hesitate to get in touch if you're at all
anxious.'

Robin wasn't absolutely sure he hadn't meant to
rebuke her by refusing tea and, keen to keep her
promotion on the popularity ladder, she swiftly
volunteered to check Mr McPhail's chest again that
evening. Unfortunately her mouth was full at the time
and blowing crumbs—one of which landed on the
shoulder of his white coat—couldn't have done anything
for her image.

He noticed for sure, but replied mildly enough, 'That
would be splendid, Miss Maxwell, though I hardly liked
to ask when you do so much overtime already.'

Was that sarcasm? Matron certainly didn't think so,
judging by the way she beamed and said wasn't it great
how quickly Robin had made herself indispensable.

Robin wasn't so sure. She pushed the question to the
back of her mind while treating her last outpatients back
at the Centre, but dredged it up for re-examination as she
changed out of uniform. Yes, sarcasm it had been, she
decided gloomily. And he was still calling her Miss
Maxwell too, when nobody else did and he himself gave
all his other colleagues their Christian names. Robin
realised she had been expecting a big step forward in

cordiality after yesterday's clearing of the air. It hadn't happened, and she was annoyed with herself for minding so much.

But the ominous lurching of her little car as she headed for the gate drove every other consideration out of mind. Sure enough, when she got out to look, both front tyres were half-way down. Somewhere on that rough road yesterday she had acquired a couple of slow punctures. That brought Rory to mind again. Hadn't he told her it often happened on these roads? Oh, drat the man! Why was he always in her thoughts? Concentrate on getting the car to the garage—happily not too far away.

Having arranged to collect it tomorrow after work, Robin headed for Black Rock on foot just as the heavens opened again. This certainly wasn't her day, but perhaps it would clear up before her evening visit to the hospital. It didn't—and next morning when she pulled back her bedroom curtains it was still bucketing down. If it went on like this, a waterlogged Vallersay could sink without trace by the end of the week!

To the hospital first, arriving wet and dripping, where Archie in expansive mood had the bright idea of getting her to do a round of the chest patients with him. Add an extended treatment for old Mr McPhail on account of the language difficulty and Robin knew she was going to be late. Crazily she chose the rhododendron path as being quicker than the drive—which it would have been, but for a generous topping of slippery mud. Even so, she only fell down once.

Rory, of course, just happened to be standing in the doorway of his room looking out for his first patient. His eyebrows rose in astonishment at the sight of Robin's bedraggled state. 'Why on earth did you not come by car on a day like this?' he wondered.

'Punctures,' she returned bitterly, sidling past so as not

to let him see her muddy backside.

His patient had arrived and he ushered him in. 'That'll teach you to go poaching on the Sabbath,' he replied with a chuckle as he closed the door.

Robin's lips had already pursed from habit. Now she released them in a surprised O. He hadn't bawled her out for being late, so things were better after all. No time to rejoice though when patients were waiting. Robin hung up her outer things to dry in the boiler-room, changed into a clean pair of uniform trousers and dashed into the department apologising profusely.

'There has to be a first time,' comforted Mrs Fraser, smiling up from her non-stop knitting. It was terribly bad for her painful neck but, being addicted to wool and needles, she refused to see the connection.

For his part, Mr Duncan guessed kindly that Robin had been kept at the hospital. She confirmed that and having fixed Mrs Fraser up for her interferential current—knitting well out of reach—she set to work on his stiff knee. 'You've done wonders in the time,' he congratulated her afterwards. 'Two months out of the plaster I was and not bending it very much by myself at all.'

Robin agreed it was amazing what a little bit of bullying could do and Mr Duncan was still denying she had done any such thing when he went off to report progress to his doctor.

Mrs Fraser was also pleased with her progress. 'You are doing me so much good, *mo ghaoil,* that I will be making you a sweater,' she threatened after Robin had spent an energetic fifteen minutes loosening her neck muscles—all as tight as whipcord when she started.

'Oh, I couldn't possibly let you do that,' breathed Robin, horrified at the idea of all her good work going to waste.

'Ach, you can be paying me for the wool,' returned Mrs Fraser, serenely misunderstanding.

Robin shook her head and smiled ruefully before turning her attention to her next patient, young Sandy from the garage and his injured hand. After Sandy came Archie's new patient of yesterday, then old Mr McKenzie—ex pier-master—bravely enduring his post-shingles pain. After him a formidable assortment of sprains, minor fractures and just for a change, a facial palsy. A rushed lunch in the staff-room with Morag, and then back to the hospital—by road this time.

Before she came, Robin foolishly imagined working days that would somehow trundle along at the leisurely pace of long-ago holidays, but Vallersay could rival anything she had known at St Crispin's. Today, she had to refuse Matron's kind offer of tea because she had an ante-natal class waiting for her back at the Centre. By then Robin could think of nothing but a leisurely bath and a nice lie down before dinner, so the cryptic note she found on her desk brought on a very heavy sigh. All it said was—Home visit today for Mrs M. F. McKenzie, leaving half five—in Rory's firm clear hand.

'No address and no diagnosis; very helpful,' she muttered, but there was no time to fill in the gaps now, because Jock's patients were already there and looking expectant in more ways than one. During their fifteen minutes of quiet relaxation at the end of their class though, Robin dashed along to Records to look up Mrs McKenzie's address. Heavens! Claddaich, the croft where she lived, was on the other side of the island near the Standing Stanes! And as if that wasn't enough, she couldn't find the lady's notes anywhere. She was being sent to visit a patient without any idea what was wrong with her and therefore no idea what equipment—if any—to take. Had Rory, the infallible, slipped up at last?

As soon as her patients had departed, Robin put together a selection of walking and other aids calculated to fit most situations. She would need her car, of course, so next she ran all the way to the garage, fuming as she went. She hoped she was as dedicated as the next girl, but surely anybody would find this too much on top of the day she'd had. Rory McEwan was the absolute end. No wonder his Deirdre had bolted.

Back at the Centre, she was astonished to see the cause of her present annoyance sitting in his Range Rover drumming impatient fingers on the steering wheel. As ever, Eorna was beside him. As Robin parked and got out, he leaned through the open window and asked, 'Could you not have left your car until tomorrow, *caileag*?'

She gasped and stared at him open-mouthed. Was he mad? How did he think she was going to manage a round trip of twenty miles or more without it? With tremendous self-control she managed to say politely, 'Yes, I know I shall be late, but I did have patients until five and, although the garage is on my way, I fetched the car along here because there is so much stuff I thought I'd better take . . .' He had been looking more and more mystified during all this, which was probably why she had a new thought. 'I must have got the wrong McKenzie,' she mumbled, flushing. Damn him—she hadn't blushed like that for years!

Now he was looking at her as if he thought she had gone off her head. 'That wouldn't be difficult when there are at least a hundred of them on the island—and they all seem to be rather unhealthy. Only I don't recall giving you an address. Which one did you have in mind?'

'Mrs McKenzie of Claddaich,' she admitted reluctantly and feeling very foolish because the only possible explanation was that she was down to visit somebody right here in town.

Yet to her utter amazement he said calmly, 'That's right, that's the one. And now for heaven's sake stop gaping at me as if you thought I was deranged and go and fetch whatever it is you're planning to take. I told the patient's daughter we'd try to be there by six.'

Robin slumped back against her little car. 'You mean—you're going too?' she asked dazedly.

'But of course! Believe me, I'd have given you far more information than I did if I'd meant you to go alone.'

Feeling every kind of a clown, Robin locked up her car with trembling fingers. Was it too much to hope he hadn't guessed what had been going through her mind? The answer was yes. When she turned round there he was, grinning from ear to ear. 'No wonder you looked so dazed when I said you needn't have gone for your car. That would have been some hike, wouldn't it? I doubt you'd have been gey late for work tomorrow—that's if you made it at all.' His rippling laughter followed her into the building.

'Damn, damn, damn, damn,' she muttered all the way to Physio. Nobody liked appearing stupid and she had made the most appalling idiot of herself—worse than she could ever remember. And in front of him, of all people! Her face was on fire with humiliation and she buried it in the pillows of the diathermy couch, beating her fists with frustration. Fancy being daft enough to think that anybody—even Rory McEwan—would expect her to walk all that way, and without knowing why or what she was supposed to do when she got there! Robin straightened up, biting her lips. No wonder he had laughed—and it was funny, she admitted reluctantly. If anybody else had made that mistake, I'd have been laughing my head off too by now. Vividly she pictured herself trudging on and on—through driving rain and half a gale of course!—and a tiny chuckle exploded in her throat. She went on chuckling softly as she picked up the bundle she'd made up earlier.

Rory was still laughing when she got back, but he suppressed his amusement when he saw her and, leaping out, he took her bundle and put it on the back seat. He opened the passenger door for her and she climbed in, not daring to look at him and trying desperately hard to appear dignified. Eorna jumped into the front to welcome her and Robin made an elaborate fuss of her, but it was no use. That woeful picture of herself on the road refused to go away. A great chuckle escaped her and she clasped a hand over her mouth.

'Would you be feeling ill at all?' Rory enquired softly from his seat beside her.

Still gurgling, Robin shook her head, then giving up the struggle she relaxed back in her seat and laughed until the tears came. That was enough to start Rory off again and the patients going in and out for evening surgery were treated to the surprising spectacle of Dr Rory and the new physio sitting there in his car, splitting their sides.

When they had calmed down, Rory slewed round in his seat and looked at Robin as if he was really seeing her for the first time. 'It's an exceptional woman who can laugh at herself like that,' he stated thoughtfully.

'Huh! If you really want to know, I felt more like ending it all at first. How stupid can one get?'

'I didn't think you were stupid. Well, not exactly. A little confused perhaps . . .'

'Don't push your luck,' she advised, lips twitching again. 'It's as much your fault as mine if I did get confused. Who ever heard of a doctor taking a physio on a home visit? It never happens at St Crispin's.'

'Come to think of it, I don't believe it happens much

in Glasgow either,' he conceded, 'but in Vallersay we make our own rules to suit our special circumstances. You'll get used to it.'

'Thanks,' she said. 'In future I'll try to remember not to be surprised at anything.' She glanced at the dashboard clock. 'Oh, dear, we're going to be late.'

'But not as late as you . . .'

'. . . as I would have been—yes, I know,' she interrupted ruefully, her pride still tender.

'Dear me, we are put out,' he reckoned in a soft, beguiling voice, such as he'd never used to her before. 'Would it help if I told you I'm beginning to understand why my partners approve of you the way they do?'

'It might—if I thought I could believe it.'

'Fasten your seat-belt,' he ordered; then with mock menace, borrowing her own phrase, 'And don't push your luck, *mo ghaoil*.' Then he ordered Eorna into the back and they set off.

Having subsided unnoticed to a gentle drizzle during all that drama, the rain ceased altogether now and the sun had won through by the time they reached the rough road that divided Vallersay in two. Clouds still clung to the mountain tops, but the lower-lying moorland was steaming gently in the heat. A grouse flew right across the car with a hoarse tck! tck! of reproof and Robin winced for its safety.

'Your sympathy is misdirected,' considered Rory, viewing with disgust its calling card plumb in the middle of his shining bonnet.

'I expect the poor thing was frightened,' she defended it.

'Is there any living thing that fails to excite your concern?' he asked with a fleeting smile.

'Oh, lots, but listing them would make me sound intolerant and that wouldn't be good for my image.'

'I like it,' he said definitely. 'A woman who's prepared to admit she's not quite perfect. What a rarity!'

'Thank you, Doctor. That has to be a compliment coming from one of the perfect sex,' returned Robin with gentle irony.

'Ouch!' exclaimed Rory with a comical grimace. 'Let's talk patients. That at least is one debate I'll not be afraid of losing.' He changed down as they approached the last steep incline. 'For a start, our Mrs Mhairi Forbes McKenzie presents us with a very complicated problem indeed.'

'For a start, she doesn't speak English,' hazarded Robin with a sigh, and delving into her bag to make sure she had her phrase book with her.

'Wrong, but wait until you hear this.' The poor lady, it transpired, had endured far more than her fair share of ill health, including diabetes, angina and a fractured hip. Now they were answering a call to deal with what sounded like a stroke. 'And before you ask me why I didn't just send the ambulance to bring her into hospital, that was my first reaction, but she refused—ostensibly because the last time she was in, her daughter couldn't visit her very often.'

'No car?'

'No time. The poor woman runs the croft virtually singlehanded since her father died.'

'Oh, dear.' Robin could sympathise with the patient's reluctance to go into hospital, but treating her at home was a daunting prospect, there being no way she could fit it in during the day.

But this wasn't what Rory had in mind. 'Actually, it's not just the lack of home contact that's putting her off,' he continued, sounding curiously reluctant. 'Last time she was in, she didn't quite hit it off with—with your predecessor and took against all physios in consequence.

I'm dragging you along tonight in the hope that you can cure that prejudice. Apart from the importance of hospitalisation to her own recovery, her daughter would be run ragged nursing her and coping with the croft—and would probably end up as a patient herself.'

'I can see what you mean about it being a complicated situation,' Robin murmured thoughtfully as they left the road and jolted slowly up a rutted track to the isolated McKenzie place.

There were several moments in the next hour or so when Robin thought they weren't going to win, but eventually all was settled and they climbed back into the Range Rover, leaving a relieved Miss Nan McKenzie— looking ten years younger than when they arrived—to pack a case for her mother and await the arrival of the ambulance.

'Well, thank Heaven for that,' breathed Rory with immense satisfaction as they bounced carefully back down the track to the main road.

'She could never have managed,' said Robin, meaning the daughter, 'and I think her mother realised it in the end.'

'Not at all. It was the rosy picture you painted of rehabilitation that did it. You made it sound like a Saturday night *céilidh*. When you made her laugh, I knew we'd won.'

'But if she hadn't understood English, it might have been a different story.'

'Not at all,' he repeated. 'Ella Crombie insists that if the Martians landed, you'd get through to them.'

'I wouldn't like to try,' she answered, with a little chuckle, and then as they reached the road she asked, 'I say, aren't we going the wrong way?'

'I'm not on call tonight, and as it's turned out to be such a marvellous evening, I thought we might as well go back by the coast road. Any objections?'

'No—none at all.' Quite the contrary. All those compliments and now the long way home—it wasn't only the weather that had improved since she made such a donkey of herself that afternoon.

'You really do know the island well, don't you?' admitted Rory some time later when he had pointed out yet another feature of interest she had seen before. 'But now for something you won't have visited.'

'The lighthouse,' she guessed confidently, when they left the main road a moment later in favour of a narrow, winding lane plunging steeply downhill between thickly planted trees.

'Wrong then, Miss Knowall,' said Rory with unmistakable glee, forestalling her hovering question by telling her to sit tight and wait and see.

At the foot of the cliff a stretch of coarse grass bordered the shore. Out to sea on a rocky reef was the lighthouse, but away to the south at the end of the track, a rambling barn had been recently restored. There were several cars parked there already.

'A folk museum,' tried Robin.

'What, open at this time in the evening? Don't be daft—you're losing your touch.' Rory squeezed the Range Rover into a space Robin would have thought impossible, then he pointed to the brightly painted sign over the door. '*An Breac Donn* means the Brown Trout. It's only been open a week just, and you are in for the gastronomic experience of your life, *mo ghaoil*.'

'How exciting,' gurgled Robin, 'but what will I say to my landlady?'

'Tell her your trip took longer than you thought. You're not afraid of her, are you?'

'No—but she is expecting me back for dinner.'

'Then ring her while I see about a table. You'll find a phone in the hall.' He'd been before then—with the haughty Selina perhaps? Well, he wasn't with Selina this time.

Having explained her lateness to Mrs McKenzie, Robin had found something else to worry about by the time she joined Rory in the tiny bar. 'I've never dined out wearing uniform before.'

'And I have never before entertained a female who showed so little enthusiasm for the experience. It's devastating.'

'But I am—enthusiastic, I mean. I just thought . . .'

With a knowing glance at her trim figure in the crisp white tunic and snugly fitting navy stretch trousers, he leaned along the bar to whisper, 'If it's any comfort to you, you look a sight more appetising than that heavyweight female over there in the pink satin blouse and overstuffed jeans.' She giggled and he handed her a tomato juice. Coincidence—or had he actually remembered that she didn't drink? 'I suggest you get outside of that and try to let your hair down a bit.' His gaze shifted to Robin's abundance of toffee-coloured curls. 'Metaphorically speaking, that is,' he added with a very good example of his singularly charming smile.

Robin smiled back. 'I'm sorry. I didn't mean to be such a drip. This is tremendously kind of you and I appreciate it very much.'

'Now you're overdoing it,' he reckoned, smiling into her eyes again.

Two such looks in quick succession—wonderful. Sipping her tomato juice, Robin marvelled at the warm glow it seemed to be imparting and a small secret smile played about her mouth.

'You should smile more often,' Rory discovered. 'It makes you look years younger and really quite pretty.'

'Well, thank you. Many more fulsome compliments like that and I might start thinking you quite like me.'

Rory drained his glass and put it back on the bar counter. 'As to that, I'm half inclined to think as much myself. Now let's eat. I hope you like lobster.'

'I'm crazy about it,' Robin assured him truthfully.

It was delicious, as was the refreshing fruit mousse which followed. They lingered over the meal, in a mood of relaxed enjoyment and accord, and when at last they wandered outside, the shadows were lengthening. Eorna whined restlessly when she saw them and Rory let her out of the car. 'She's been penned up all day, the *caileag*,' he said. 'Do you mind if we give her a run on the beach?'

The dog was already bounding joyfully in that direction and Robin suggested with a smile that they didn't seem to have much choice.

Except for Eorna, now well ahead, they were quite alone on the shore. The sandy strip above the water-line was firm and pleasant underfoot. It was also rather narrow and as they walked closely side by side, their hands brushed together more than once. So it seemed inevitable that Rory's should eventually close over Robin's. They strolled on.

She was acutely conscious of her hand lying in his—and of the strength of her longing to return its pressure. Suddenly his hand crushed her fingers tight and she started confusedly, thinking at first he had read her thoughts. 'Look,' he whispered, pointing to the shallows some way ahead. There two otters were playing—rolling, twisting and nipping at each other. They stood quite still, both enchanted, until Eorna burst out of cover and plunged into the water. The otters swam off at speed, their heads carving lengthening arrows through the calm, twinkling sea. 'Not a lot of that sort of thing to be seen in a city,' Rory breathed in her ear.

Hardly aware of responding so, Robin leaned against him. 'That was sheer magic.'

'A fair exchange, then?'

'How can you ask? There is simply no contest.'

She couldn't have told just how it happened, but next minute she was in his arms and his mouth was on hers, satisfying and sweet. But even as her eager arms stole round his taut muscular body, he released her. When he didn't speak, Robin murmured, 'And to think that just days ago we were quarrelling.'

Rory chuckled softly deep in his throat. 'This has to be an improvement—as long as . . .' he hesitated. 'That was rather a rapid progression, I'm thinking.'

It was, and now he is telling me not to read too much into it, she realised intuitively. 'The night and the moon and the music—only for music, read otters,' she said, moving away from him with a contrived little laugh. 'Didn't I say something about magic?'

'You did and you're not wrong.' She could have sworn there was relief in his voice. He took her hand again, this time in a loose, comradely grip, and they strolled back to the car.

Relieved? Perhaps, but he was exhilarated all the same. He entertained her with comic island tales all the way back to Bratanport and when he parked his car beside hers at the Centre they were both almost as helpless with laughter as they had been when they set out. Eorna, disgusted at being ignored, had gone to sleep on the back seat.

Robin found her hankie and wiped her eyes as she struggled for calm. 'You really ought to write a book about Vallersay—it'd be a riot.'

'There'd be a riot right enough—and my fellow islanders would very likely lynch me for a finale.'

'Then I take it all back,' Robin said quickly.

'Well, thank you.' He stretched his arms behind his head, then relaxed with a small sigh. 'I suppose you'll be wanting to go and make your peace with Mrs McKenzie now.'

It would be nice to think he was as reluctant for the evening to end as she was. 'I suppose I'd better. She's terribly kind but sometimes she makes me feel—smothered.'

'Wouldn't you feel freer in a place of your own?'

'That's for sure, but there's not much hope of that until the season is over, I'm afraid. I only wish there were; my parents are longing to visit Vallersay again, now they're back in Edinburgh.'

'Something may turn up,' he returned encouragingly.

'I hope so—apart from anything else, I'm putting on weight at a terrible rate, thanks to Mrs Mac's splendid cuisine.'

There was just enough light from the moon and the street lamps for Rory to scan her thoroughly. 'Everything looks fine to me,' he decided.

'You're only saying that to keep me sweet,' she challenged, opening the door and jumping down.

Rory leapt out too and opened the door of her own car for her. Then with his hands on her shoulders he said, 'Not so. If a doctor doesn't know how the female form should look, who does?' He drew her casually towards him and kissed her very lightly on the cheek. 'Thanks for a really super evening, Robin.'

'You've just stolen my exit line,' she returned unsteadily. 'I haven't enjoyed myself so much for ages.'

Rory left her with a little laugh and got back in his car. 'Vallersay one, London nil, then,' he called carelessly as he drove away.

CHAPTER SIX

'YOU are very cheerful for a *caileag* who is working such long hours,' considered her landlady when Robin came humming into breakfast next morning.

'But I enjoy my work, Mrs Mac.'

'That is good, but all this overtime.' She shook her head. 'It iss not right. I am surprised at Dr Rory.'

Not half as much as you would be if you knew *all*, thought Robin with an inward chuckle. 'He was working overtime himself last night,' she returned demurely as she started on her grapefruit.

Mrs McKenzie put down the coffee-pot with a thump and stated firmly, 'That iss different. He iss a man.' Remembering the way she had felt in his arms last night, Robin couldn't possibly have disagreed with that.

She raced through breakfast and drove to work for quickness. Having given Mrs M. F. McKenzie such a rosy picture of getting better the Maxwell way, it seemed only sensible to get her started as soon as possible. Treatment for the chestiest patients next and then she was hurtling back down the hill to the Centre, where she beat Mrs Campbell to the department by a whisker—much to that lady's obvious disappointment.

Her treatment completed and a grudging admission of slight improvement extracted, Robin was just helping her into her jacket when Rory walked in with the bundle of aids she had left in his car the night before. He dealt patiently with Mrs Campbell's involved recital of her newest symptoms, then when she had gone he said sympathetically, 'Poor lady. If only somebody could come up with a cure for loneliness, most of her symptoms would disappear overnight.' He dumped his load on the nearest plinth. 'I thought you might be needing these.'

'Thanks,' she responded, beaming at him. 'We were having so much fun last night that I completely forgot them.'

'Not to worry. Did you manage to have a word with our new patient up at the hospital this morning, Robin?'

'Better than that, I gave her her first treatment.'

He whistled. 'Great—you are a fast worker.' He turned to go, then asked, 'Could you possibly get old man McPhail up for a walk this afternoon? He'll probably resist like blazes, but I'm sure you'll manage to make him understand it's doctor's orders. Well, I'd better be off—see you.'

He was away before she could answer and she stared after him, conscious of a slight feeling of disappointment. Though a great improvement on one-time watchful disapproval, she had been expecting something more than mere casual friendliness—despite the warning giving last night of his intention to avoid involvement. And he'd quite ignored her reference to their happy evening together. Prudence, perhaps? All the cubicle curtains were drawn, so he wasn't to know there were no patients in just then.

As the morning wore on, it produced more than its fair share of minor problems, which required all Robin's attention. It was the same at the hospital in the afternoon. Rory, she guessed, could well be having a few problems of his own with Hamish on holiday, but she was hoping he would still find time for tea in Matron's office later. He didn't and, having lingered as long as she could afford to, she had to leave, disappointed. Snap out of it, do, she scolded herself as she returned to the Centre to complete her day. You're as bad as any lovesick schoolgirl. Love?

Robin swiftly amended that to crush!

Rory was in the waiting-room chatting to a huge bearded Viking of a man. He moved aside with a brief smile to let her by, but the stranger wasn't having that. 'Aren't you going to introduce me?' he asked reproachfully.

Rory shrugged and laid a delaying hand on Robin's shoulder. 'Fergus McInnes, an old friend—Robin Maxwell, my new physiotherapist,' he said, sounding both wary and possessive.

The Viking seized Robin's hand firmly and pumped it up and down with painful enthusiasm. 'Amazing that we haven't run into each other before,' he considered. 'Better late than never though. How are you enjoying Vallersay?'

'Very much—but then I always did.' Robin managed to free her hand as he went on to ask where she was staying.

When she said at Black Rock, he let out a long low whistle. 'You NHS folk must be paid a lot better than the media would have us believe then.'

Robin smiled wryly. 'Black Rock is superb,' she admitted, 'but I'm only there until I can find a cottage I can afford.'

Fergus McInnes flashed her a brilliant smile. 'Then your search is over. I've got the very thing for you. Why didn't you tell me this charming young lady needed accommodation?' he demanded of Rory.

Rory's eyebrows rose. 'Probably because you've always insisted you were only interested in the holiday trade,' he retorted crisply, leaving Robin with the distinct impression that wasn't his only reason.

'Ah, but I'm always prepared to make an exception in a worthy cause.'

'I couldn't afford to pay holiday prices, I'm afraid,' Robin put in quickly, noting Rory's nod of agreement.

Just as promptly, Fergus suggested a sum that was

barely half what she'd been paying in London, following that with an offer to call back and take her to see the cottage as soon as she finished work.

'I couldn't put you to so much trouble when I have my car right here,' she declined gracefully. 'But if I could have the address . . .' She pulled out her notebook to take it down, recognising the name of a farm on the hill behind the Andersons' house. It was all arranged before she met Rory's frowning glance, but her next patient was just coming in so there was no time to wonder why he disapproved, after agreeing only yesterday that she'd be better off in a cottage.

There was just time to fix Mrs Scott up for diathermy to her back before Rory appeared in the doorway. With a jerk of the head he invited her to step into the corridor out of earshot. 'About that cottage,' he opened. 'One thing is sure, you'd not find a nicer one anywhere else, but Fergus himself could turn out to be a problem. He simply cannot resist making a pass at every pretty girl he meets.' With a crooked little smile he added, 'Could be you noticed that, though.'

'He's certainly very friendly—and most accommodating.' She was thinking of the modest rent he was asking.

Rory gave a shout of laughter. 'And that's a priceless way of describing him. It's up to you of course, but as your boss with your welfare at heart, I felt obliged to point out the possible drawback.' Again that grin. 'You may feel you've already had enough—aggravation from the islanders.'

What *did* he mean? Please, not last night's interlude on the beach!

'I'm sure your friend is too much of a gentleman to persist with unwanted attentions, so I'm not too worried about that.' Now how best to tell him something much more important? 'And as to our initial differences, I've quite forgotten them.'

This time she got a full-scale smile. 'Splendid,' he said, 'but I mustn't hold you up any more. Let me know what you decide, won't you?'

'Of course,' she agreed hurriedly, before dashing to answer Mrs Scott's call that she was feeling just a wee bittie too warm. Having readjusted the intensity, Robin sat down to consider that conversation, coming reluctantly to the conclusion that she was no nearer guessing his present attitude towards her than she had been before.

Robin's last patient of the day lived in one of the new houses quite near to Lindsay and Jock, so Robin offered her a lift home. Unlike most islanders, who never gossiped about each other to an incomer, this lady was bursting with information about Fergus McInnes. By the time Robin dropped her off, she knew all about Fergus's problems with his unproductive farm, which had resulted in his selling off most of it for housing. Recently, he had converted all his outbuildings into holiday cottages. 'And I am hearing they are very smart,' was the patient's parting comment.

Rory had praised them too, so Robin drove the rest of the way in a state of pleasurable anticipation. Her expectations were more than met. The living-room was large and raftered, with a rustic stone fireplace and a large picture window looking right over Bratanport to the sea. A tiny pine-panelled kitchen occupied a recess and off an even tinier inner hall were two little bedrooms and a shower-room. The décor was a nice blend of heather and Habitat, and Robin could hardly believe her luck. She felt obliged to query the rent Fergus had quoted, though, but he insisted it was ample for a long-term let. They concluded the bargain over a long, cool drink in his ultra-modern kitchen at the farmhouse, with Fergus behaving impeccably. She arranged to move in when the present tenants left at the end of the month.

Some of Robin's euphoria had evaporated by the time she got back to Black Rock. Whatever had been said, she felt sure that Mrs McKenzie had come to regard her as a fixture for the season; might even have refused some bookings on her account. Now that was a facer. A pity I don't drink, thought Robin. Right now, I could do with a Dougal-sized dram.

As Robin crossed the hall, Mrs McKenzie stepped out of the guests' phone booth to intercept her. 'It's Dr Rory for you. I hope he is not wanting you to go back to work,' she added.

He wasn't. He had rung up to hear what she had decided about the cottage and Robin made sure the door was shut tight before telling him she had taken it.

'Couldn't resist it, eh? I thought that's how it would be. Well, don't say I didn't warn you.'

'I won't, but somehow I don't think the problem will arise.'

'I hope I know how to take that,' he said puzzlingly, but before she could ask for enlightenment young Flora began her nightly assault on the dinner-gong, and, the minute she stopped, Rory said he had to hurry now, and put the phone down.

The minute dinner was over, Robin went to confess her coming desertion to Mrs McKenzie, only to discover that the Vallersay telegraph had got in first. 'Flora is second cousin to the *caileag* who does for Mr McInnes, so when we heard you were going to see one of his wee places, I felt sure you would take it.'

'I hope I'm not inconveniencing you at all,' offered Robin.

'No, not at all. Miss Gordon who comes for the month of August every year always has your room, so now I will not be having to ask you to change rooms!' She regarded Robin sternly over the tops of her glasses. 'You will be feeding yourself properly, I am hoping.'

'Oh, yes—but not as well as you do, of course,' was the truth as well as being eminently tactful.

'Isn't it strange how the things you fret and worry about most never turn out to be as bad as you expected,' she said to Dougal when they met by arrangement at the Smugglers' Rest about an hour later.

He had her favourite soft drink ready and waiting and he pushed it across the table towards her. 'I never worry about anything, yet I lurch from crisis to crisis all the time,' he returned wryly. 'So what brought on that attack of philosophy, Rob? Is Rory McEwan still driving you nuts?'

'No—he seems to have turned over a new leaf.' She told Dougal all about the cottage. 'I was dreading telling my landlady and it turned out that my going actually suits her very well. That's what I was meaning. She's been so motherly that I thought she'd be upset.' She remembered Rory's warning. 'By the way, Dougal, do you know anything about Fergus McInnes?'

Dougal pulled thoughtfully at his straggly beard. 'He's a very amiable chap—generous too; always stands his round and then some.' He chuckled. 'He's a great one for the lassies and has broken plenty of hearts in his time. You'll need to watch him, Rob.'

'More or less what Rory McEwan said.'

'You're well warned then.' But Dougal had some news of his own. 'I sold two paintings today, Robin.'

'Oh, Dougal, that's marvellous. Enough to get your roof repaired?' she asked practically.

'Enough to allow me to drink malt instead of blended for a year or two. Which reminds me, there's just time for another.'

Robin smiled resignedly as she watched him lounge over to the bar. He had tidied himself up somewhat since they'd met again, but she doubted if he'd ever develop a sense of responsibility. Yet he seemed completely happy with his life, and how many people could say that?

The Smugglers' Rest boasted an excellent restaurant and Robin was diverted from thoughts of her unconventional friend by a great deal of laughter outside as a party of late diners emerged. Idly she pulled back the curtain and peered out. Quite a large mixed party it was—and in the middle of it, Rory with Selina Stuart-Strang. He seemed to be having difficulty keeping her upright.

She's drunk, thought Robin, disgust replacing her initial dismay. Well, if that was the way he liked his women to behave when he took them out, then she simply didn't stand a chance.

The revellers were still outside when she and Dougal left soon after and by then Rory was bundling Selina rather roughly into the Range Rover. 'Goodnight, Dr McEwan—Miss Stuart-Strang,' fluted Robin in passing, causing Selina to miss her footing and collapse giggling to the ground. Dougal sniggered and Rory turned round to glare at him. Robin strode on in dismay. So nothing had been changed by yesterday's wonderful evening, and having Rory know she had witnessed his girlfriend's loss of dignity was hardly any comfort.

She had been so sure that he would take care to ward off any comments about it that she was absolutely astounded when he said right out of the blue next morning, 'You'll be glad to hear that Selina was none the worse after her fall last night, Robin.'

It had been a busy morning, and it was nearly twelve before she had time to dash to the kitchen for a quick cup of instant coffee. She'd believed that all the doctors would have had theirs long since and be away on their rounds, so hearing Rory say that right behind her was so startling that she slopped half her coffee over into her saucer, scalding her thumb as well. She sucked it, then whirled round, spilling some more. 'Oh, good,' she managed weakly.

'Yes, I knew you'd be glad to know you won't be getting another patient when you're so busy. Allow me.' Calmly he relieved her of the mess she was holding and made some more for them both.

Robin watched speechless, amazed at his self-possession. 'Thank you,' she said automatically on being presented with a fresh coffee. The kitchen was small and she was suddenly very aware of his nearness. She watched him ladling sugar into his coffee, then raised her eyes to his face as he lifted the cup to his lips. His grey eyes glinted disturbingly in response and she shifted her gaze to the poster listing calorific values hanging up over the sink.

'Yesterday was her birthday and she'd only had a small sherry and two glasses of Bordeaux,' Rory continued not so very far from Robin's left ear. 'But the silly *caileag* had been helping herself to her aunt's anti-depressants on the quiet. Hence the floor show.'

Robin forced herself to concentrate on his words and not his physical presence. So that was to be the explanation, was it? Very neat. 'I wouldn't have expected anybody of Miss Stuart-Strang's . . . er . . . vitality to need anti-depressants.'

'All that effervescence is just a blind—she's actually rather a sad, introspective sort of girl.'

'Is she? One would never have guessed,' Robin returned, remembering the clever way Selina had dealt with any possible pretensions of her own on finding her in Rory's sitting-room last Sunday.

'Selina hasn't had her troubles to seek, but she does conceal it well, doesn't she?' he persisted. 'It might be better for her if she didn't. People are inclined to condemn her unfairly.'

Robin positively snorted. Was he totally infatuated? 'Just as they do Dougal McKnight, perhaps? Only he doesn't have such—trusting friends.' She had very nearly said doting!

Instead of looking abashed as he was supposed to, Rory merely grinned. 'Well, you said it,' he pointed out with relish, just as she realised herself what an opening she had handed him. 'Incidentally, do you have anything on tonight?' his voice had dropped to a caressing whisper.

'Yes, I have, as a matter of fact.' She hadn't, but Robin was in no mood to oblige him by taking on anything that wasn't absolutely necessary, and it had to be work he was thinking of, didn't it?

He shrugged, looking quite disappointed. 'Ah, well, it can't be helped.' Nothing vital then. 'I'd better be off, I suppose. I promised Ella to do a round at one and I've a couple of visits to make first.' A friendly smile and then he put down his cup and made for the door.

Robin finished her coffee and listened to his retreating footsteps. Anti-depressants indeed. Sad and introspective! Amazing how otherwise sensible and capable men could make such fools of themselves over women. It was David and Marcia all over again. Was she fated to spend her whole life on the sidelines, watching every man who attracted her chasing after somebody else? Now there was a thought calculated to take the shine off any girl's day, but she hadn't time to examine it. Rory McEwan wasn't the only one with a tight schedule to keep.

Just when Robin thought she'd finished for the morning, Morag came dashing into Physio red-faced and breathless. 'Oh, Robin—a dreadful thing. A poor old lady has fallen over on the beach and can't get up again!'

'Lead the way.' Robin followed Morag at the double and found the casualty down near the water's edge. It was obvious from the awkward position in which she lay that her hip was broken. Robin sent Morag to phone for the ambulance and squatted down beside the patient to hold her hand and reassure her. By the time the ambulance came, it was time Robin was at the hospital herself, so she rode along with the old lady and her anxious husband.

The women's ward was already full, so Robin had to start her treatments that afternoon amid a flurry of activity as the nurses looked out and assembled one of the old beds kept in store for just this type of emergency. The women were excited by all the bustle.

'It iss just like the Glasgow Royal, I am thinking,' considered that Mrs McKenzie who kept the Bratanport baker's shop.

Robin wondered how soon Rory would be able to operate and tried not to hope that this emergency would put paid to another evening out with the laird's daughter. How petty could one get? She gave herself a reproving little mental shake and concentrated on training Mrs Claddaich McKenzie's balance reactions. Here she was helped enormously by her patient's dogged determination to sit up as straight as possible so as not to miss any of the excitement.

Sister Urquhart was off duty, so it was Ella herself who supervised their new patient's transfer to her hospital bed. 'Jock will take evening surgery to leave Rory and Archie free to operate as soon after five as possible,' she explained in answer to Robin's query about timing. 'Would you mind checking her chest, Robin? And come straight to my room after you finish,' she added severely when Robin's stomach loudly announced its disgust at not being given lunch. 'I'm tired of telling you not to miss your meals.'

Robin had no objection to obeying—it was a long time until dinner—and she was on her second scone when Rory joined them. 'Glad to see not everybody is rushed off their feet today,' he observed maddeningly. 'I don't suppose you've managed to pre-op our new patient?' he added, fixing Robin with what she could only call a provocative look.

She all but choked in her hurry to say, 'Oh, yes, I have—and her chest is quite clear. And incidentally, she tells me she's never had a day's illness in her life.'

'Wonderful. It's a pity we don't have full lab facilities here—I'd give a lot to analyse the antibodies of such a healthy lady.' Hurriedly he drank half a cup of tea and took the last scone. 'My lunch,' he said with exaggerated pathos.

'I didn't have any either,' retorted Robin, but by then he was out of the door.

'What a man,' observed Ella admiringly.

'I couldn't agree more,' said Robin, while doubting they both meant that in the same way.

Having checked the new patient's chest that evening and found it to be still clear, Robin strolled back down the hill. It was just such another lovely evening as Tuesday's and she found herself savouring that wonderful evening all over again. Damn the man! Why did it matter so much? Why must she always hanker after the unattainable? As an antidote, she tried to remember how much she had disliked him at first, but now it was impossible to imagine.

Early next morning, Rory came to see their newest patient just as Robin was settling her down again after treatment. 'Hold on a minute,' he said, 'and I'll walk down the hill with you.'

'All right.' She stood at the foot of the bed and watched

as he sounded Mrs Scobie's chest and examined her operation wound. He was calm, competent and very reassuring. Robin found herself noticing other things too—like the way his thick brown hair curled at the base of his skull, the white evenness of his teeth, the uncompromising jawline, the strong cord of the sterno-mastoid muscle in his bronzed neck.

'Anything amiss?' he asked suddenly, startling her out of this rapt contemplation.

She coloured. 'Sorry—I was miles away.'

The examination over, he bade Mrs Scobie good morning, and as they moved towards the door he said softly, 'I thought for sure I must have forgotten to wash behind my ears. Unless of course you were admiring me.'

Safely in the corridor and quite scarlet now, Robin still managed to say firmly, 'You are the most conceited man I ever met.'

'I know—but it is my only fault.'

'Since when?'

'Whatever can you mean?' he asked, opening the front door.

'If I told you, you'd probably sack me on the spot.'

'Then forget I asked.' They went in Indian style down the rhododendron path in silence, but just before they reached the Centre Rory asked in a gentle voice, 'Is anything the matter, Robin?'

'No, nothing. Why?'

'You're different. Remote. What happened to the bubbly girl I discovered just the other day?'

Robin sent him a reproachful glance under her thick lashes. 'Could be she only pops out when she makes a fool of herself,' she countered.

'Then that is a great pity, because I get the feeling she doesn't do that very often.'

'She tries not to—it's so bad for the ego,' she said as

they parted in the waiting-room of the Centre.

Unlike yesterday, the morning went smoothly and Robin even had time to talk to her patients more—an unusual luxury they all enjoyed. The afternoon went well too, only marred by Mrs Scobie's spiking a temperature, which on balance suggested an incipient chest infection. 'I'll be back to see her this evening, Sister,' promised Robin on leaving. There was no tea in the office today, with Ella taking her usual Friday off, and she hadn't seen Rory again since the morning.

'I never knew such a *caileag* for the work,' considered Mrs Claddaich McKenzie when Robin walked into the ward just before nine. 'When I was here before with my broken hip, a body could have choked to death before *that one* would have come and helped you, I'm thinking.'

Gross slander brought on by personal dislike, hoped Robin, deciding it was best to ignore this slur on her predecessor's reputation. Mrs Scobie meanwhile was making it quite clear she felt all this attention quite superfluous. She changed her mind though after coughing up a thick plug of mucus which the night nurse assured her had probably saved her from a collapsed lung. 'I'm sorry if I was short with you, dear,' she apologised to Robin. 'I expect it comes of never having been ill before.'

'Think nothing of it,' Robin soothed her. 'I hate to think what I'd say to a physiotherapist who kept coming and pummelling my chest when I'd just had an operation. Anyway, you'll be allowed to sit out of bed tomorrow and then you shouldn't have any more trouble.'

Having said goodnight all round, she left the ward— then was surprised to find Rory outside in earnest conversation with the night sister. He swung round on hearing her step and his face lit up with his attractive smile. 'Have you ever assisted at an operation?' he demanded urgently.

'Only orthopaedic ones,' she answered, trying not to mind that his pleasure at seeing her was apparently professional rather than personal.

'As I expected,' he sighed. 'The thing is, Robin, we've just got this chap in off one of the yachts. Acute appendix. I'm going to whip it out as soon as Archie gets here to put him under, but Sister was just telling me she is very short of nurses tonight and we could do with another pair of hands in theatre.'

'Well, if you're that desperate, I don't mind staying on and doing what I'm told—but I'll need telling, mind.'

'Good lass. And it shouldn't take more than ten minutes.'

If only St Crispin's could see me now, thought Robin as, scrubbed up and gowned, she stood at Rory's side to hand him the instruments he pointed to. He was just as quick as he had promised—and deft too. His concentration was absolute and the only unnecessary comment he made was to say grimly, 'Not a moment too soon,' as he deposited the grossly inflamed appendix on the rubbish tray.

'You've got to admit there's nothing routine or dull about working in Vallersay, Robin,' challenged Archie as they washed afterwards, having sent their patient back to the ward to sleep it off.

She chuckled. 'Any day now I expect to be detailed to dish out bedpans—or take over from the cook.'

'Talking of cooking,' said Rory with a thoughtful gleam in his eye, 'we usually have a cuppa in the office when we've been in theatre, but tonight—with the nursing shortage . . .'

'All right, I can take a hint,' she said. 'But just watch out that I don't report you both to the Equal Opportunities Commission.'

When she carried the tea-tray into Ella's room five

minutes later, Rory was there alone. 'I fetched Archie out of a dinner party,' he explained, lounging back in Ella's chair with his feet up on her desk.

Robin was sharply reminded of their first meeting. She had thought him unprofessional and slack then, but she knew better now. Silently she poured his tea and handed it to him. 'They'll love welcoming him smelling of antiseptic, I don't think.'

'They'll love it anyway—and press him for all the gory details too, probably. Funny how the general public always thinks a doctor's life is so glamorous. They should try it at four o'clock on a frosty winter's morning when the car won't start and you've got a cold coming on.'

'Did you never think of doing something else?' asked Robin, while fairly sure she knew the answer.

'Never—not once.' He smiled crookedly. 'Bred in the bone, I suppose.'

'I can see that, but why Vallersay?'

'Why not? It's my home and our people have as much right to be cared for as folk in the town. Anyway, I hate towns.' He drained his cup and passed it over for a refill. 'You asked me why Vallersay. Now I'm asking you the same question.'

She'd walked right into that one. Would he notice if she only told him half the truth? 'I was feeling—rather fed up with St Crispin's; not the hospital, but the powers that be. I'd been more or less promised the senior post on Orthopaedics and then they went and gave it to an outsider—they *said* it was because as a married man with a child he needed the promotion more than me. I felt sort of let down and ill-used.' She hesitated. 'Funnily enough, I got a letter from my ex-boss just yesterday, telling me that the man has already applied for a superintendent's post somewhere else.'

Rory scowled and in a single movement, removed his

feet from the desk and leaned forward. 'Are you leading up to telling me you want to go back there?'

'No way! Serve them right—they backed the wrong horse and now they can jolly well live with the consequences.'

His face broke into a smile as he reached across the desk to squeeze her hand. 'That's the spirit, and sticking to the equine metaphors, I'd like to say that Vallersay's dark horse has turned out to be a thoroughbred and I for one mean to make it very difficult for her to canter out on us.'

'Dear me, that sounds rather like a threat,' returned Robin demurely. 'And how are you going to do that, may I ask?'

He relaxed back again, hands behind his head, and smiled at her impishly. 'Easty. If you try to escape, I shall blacken your character to such a degree that no hospital in Europe—never mind Scotland—will take you. I hold all the aces.'

'Not quite.'

He gave her a ferocious glare. 'How come?'

'They know me so well at St Crispin's that they'd never believe you.'

'But you've only just said you wouldn't go back there after the way they treated you.'

'I wouldn't want to—but I would if nobody else would have me.'

'So I've not got quite the hold on you I thought. I can see I shall have to be very nice to you in future.'

'Very nice indeed,' amended Robin firmly.

He stared into her eyes for a teasing moment before saying, 'Since there's nothing like striking while the iron's hot, how about if I start tomorrow by taking you out to dinner again?'

Robin quite forgot that she usually met Dougal on Saturdays—and all about Selina too.

'I'm inclined to think that's a very good idea,' she agreed, eyes dancing.

'Great,' he answered in a satisfied way. 'And now that's settled, we'd better be moving or Sister will wonder what we're doing in here for so long.'

Outside in the cool night air, though, he was in less of a hurry. When Robin would have got into her car, he blocked her way with an arm across the door. Very seriously he said, 'Look, Robin. This may sound inconsistent, coming right after asking you out, but I feel bound to tell you that in my experience, mixing professional and personal relationships can be—pretty disastrous.'

'That's my experience too,' honesty obliged her to admit. 'And yet . . .'

He interrupted her. 'Yet you and I seem to be getting along so well now that . . . Oh, hell! What I'm trying to say is this. We enjoy each other's company, so surely if we keep it light—avoid any unreal expectations—where's the harm?'

'Put like that, I'm inclined to agree.' Yet how could a girl keep from having expectations of a man whose kisses had proved as exciting as his?

Rory put a friendly arm round her shoulders and pulled her near enough to be kissed on the cheek. 'Good. Now we really do understand each other.' He squeezed her shoulder. 'Wear your best dress tomorrow and I'll pick you up at Black Rock at seven.'

'Right you are, boss. Anything you say, boss,' she agreed lightly, since light was the way he wanted it.

She was rewarded with a burst of chuckling laughter as she drove away.

CHAPTER SEVEN

WHEN she was ready, Robin took a last look at herself in the dressing-table mirror. For once, her newly washed curls were behaving well and twined in little tendrils all round her face—elfin was how David had once described that particular look. Extra mascara and eyeshadow made her blue eyes, already generous, look huge. She'd always had a good skin. Nowhere near the polished perfection of Selina Stuart-Strang, but not bad—not bad at all. Put on your best dress, Rory had said, so she had looked out the simple but wickedly expensive cream silk she had worn at her sister's wedding, pinning on her good cameo brooch.

It being nearly Black Rock's own dinner time, Mrs McKenzie was safely busy in her kitchen at the back when Rory came. He strode up the path looking lithe and cool in a lightweight summer suit. His eyes widened with approval as she came down the steps. 'We don't see many dresses like that in Vallersay,' he commented.

Except, of course, on the laird's daughter. Twice in five minutes? Going on like that could ruin the evening, so forget her—and for goodness' sake, keep it light! 'How kind you are. And to think I nearly didn't bring it, but then I was always an optimist.'

'I'm glad I was able to justify the optimism.'

'Hm!' She paused to let that apparent doubt sink in. 'Best dress, you said—and I always try to please the boss.'

Rory chuckled. 'Do you now? Since when?' He opened the passenger door of the Range Rover.

Robin climbed in, then considered that, head on one side.

'Since always, but I'm trying much harder now that the boss is trying to please me.'

He swung himself into the driver's seat beside her. 'And are there any limits beyond which you will not go in order to please?'

There was a certain something in his voice as he said that! 'I like to keep within the law and—er—common sense.'

He laughed delightedly. 'Robin, you're a real tonic. Why were you not snapped up years ago?'

'I was spoiled for choice,' she returned drolly.

'That I can well believe.' Where she had expected uproarious laughter, he had sounded quite sincere. He started the engine and headed south. As the powerful car took the steep hill out of the town, Robin wondered where they were going, but before she could ask she noticed two women gossiping at a garden gate. In a flash she had undone her seat-belt, thrown her pink jacket over her head and slid right down in her seat.

'I suppose there was some point to all that,' observed Rory after a minute.

Cautiously she emerged from cover and resumed the upright. 'Mrs Campbell. Didn't you see her?'

'Sure. We waved to each other. She was looking gey startled, I thought.'

'You're making that up,' she guessed confidently. 'But just think what would have happened if she'd recognised me.'

'It would have been all round the island by daybreak.'

'Exactly! I was only trying to obey your rule about being careful in a small community.'

'Don't be offensive. That rule only applies to ill-chosen companions. In my company you are above reproach. Besides, we might have been going to visit a patient.'

'What—dressed like this?'

'Why not, if it were an emergency? Think of Archie and

his dinner party last night.'

'You've got an answer for everything, haven't you?'

'Not quite, but I'm working on it.'

'Where are we going?' she remembered to ask.

'What, run out of repartee, have you?' He ducked as she raised a playful fist. 'All right, I'll take that back. We are going, *mo ghaoil*, to Bracken Lodge.'

'How exciting. I've heard of it but never been there.'

'Everybody in Britain has heard of it. It's the Mecca of all dedicated anglers.'

'And I thought we were going out to dinner,' she returned with a mock sigh.

'Ha—ha—ha, very funny. Just for that I've a good mind to turn round and take you for haggis and chips at Fratini's.'

'Not that,' she pleaded. 'My hips would never stand it. I promise to be very good from now on.'

'I wish I had a sworn copy of that,' said Rory, bringing the car to a halt and letting two others go past in the opposite direction before swinging across the road.

'I've always wondered what lay behind that wall,' said Robin as they passed under an imposing stone archway into a well-kept gravel drive.

'Those for one thing.' He pointed to a herd of tame red deer grazing unhurriedly in a rough meadow beyond the inevitable hedge of wild rhododendrons.

'I've never seen so many all together before,' she breathed, leaning towards him to get a closer look.

Obligingly he slowed down. 'Then you've not been on the Claddaich moor. We must go there some Sunday.'

'I usually spend my Sundays with Calum,' she reminded him.

'So? Calum is my friend too, remember.'

'That'll be nice, but I had this idea you were more a man for climbing.'

'I haven't climbed for—some time now,' he returned shortly. He must have realised he'd sounded strange, because he added hurriedly in a much warmer tone, 'Just never seem to get the time on a suitable day. Look, Robin, there's the house.'

It was old; long, low and freshly white-washed with a multitude of dormer windows jutting out of a steep slated roof. They were greeted in the hall by the proprietor, a cheerful courteous man who had been at university with Rory. 'Be prepared for a surprise or two,' Rory whispered in her ear as they entered the bar. It was full of the kind of people who regularly made the newspapers and in seconds Robin had identified a judge, a captain of industry and a veteran actor-knight. The women were all incredibly elegant, and Robin's dress, which had cost her a painful three figures, was the cheapest in the room by far.

'So this is where the top people come for their holidays,' she murmured as she and Rory took possession of the only two vacant stools at the bar. She wondered why he had brought her.

'Impressed?' he asked, smiling.

'Very much so.'

'That's what I intended. Nothing like starting off on the right foot.'

'Starting off—what, may I ask?'

He passed her a tall glass of fruit punch with a guileless look. 'The evening of course.'

'Then that's all right,' she answered, quite thrilled to note the momentary flicker of disappointment in his deep-set grey eyes.

The dining-room was as unpretentious as the rest of the place, but the meal was exquisite: smoked Tay salmon, lamb cutlets, raspberry mousse and Caboc cheese. Scottish fare at its deceptively simple best—eaten at leisure, between the laughing exchanges that were coming so easily to them now.

Afterwards, they strolled along the banks of the trout-rich river, which pursued a twisted, whispering way gently downhill to the sea—never far away in Vallersay. Eventually the path was barred by a wooden gate. They leaned against it in quiet and intimate accord. It was no surprise to Robin when Rory reached out and pulled her against him. Had he changed his mind about keeping it light? Just in case, she murmured, 'I don't recall anything being said about this.'

'Shut up and concentrate,' he murmured against her mouth. He was expert, no doubt about that, and Robin thrilled to the feel of his gentle, questing lips, his arms about her and the pressure of his hard masculine outline. If only it weren't for that nagging little voice at the back of her mind . . .

Rory lifted his head. 'I can't help feeling you're not giving your whole attention to this,' he whispered in gentle reproach.

'I'm—confused,' she whispered back. 'We were supposed to be keeping it light, remember?'

Gently he nibbled the lobe of her left ear. 'The main trouble with you, *mo ghaoil*, is your memory. It's too damn good.'

'I expect time will sort that,' she managed with a tremulous little laugh. She yearned to let herself go, but simply didn't dare. Her recent hurt was just that—too recent. And what of his? Wasn't she just another anodyne—like, or maybe even for, Selina.

He claimed her mouth again in more bittersweet kisses and this time she couldn't help but respond, hardly knowing whether she was glad or sorry when eventually the sound of laughter and the scuffing of feet on gravel caused them to draw apart.

The couple approaching recognised Rory, despite the

gathering dusk of a late summer evening, and they passed with a cheerful greeting. Rory responded in a tone of barely concealed irritation, which Robin thought must be due to anger at being found there like that—with her. Had he thought that so far from Bratanport they might have escaped discovery? Was that then the real reason he had brought her here? After all, he usually took Selina to places in the town, didn't he? Hardly aware of it, Robin started back along the path towards the hotel. Rory followed but soon took her hand to pull her arm through his and hold it close. Comforting, but at the same time disturbing.

They couldn't go all the way back to Bratanport in silence though and as they got into the car Robin said, 'Poor Eorna is missing her run on the beach tonight.'

'I took her for a long hike this afternoon, so she'll be flat out in front of the stove, I don't doubt.'

'She must need a lot of exercise,' she persisted.

'More than she gets, I'm thinking.'

'Aren't you on duty tomorrow with Hamish away? I could look after her if you like,' she offered.

'Could you really? She'd love that.' He reached out and gently squeezed her hand. 'You're a very sweet and thoughtful girl, Robin. I'm sorry I was so—difficult at first.'

'So am I, but you're certainly making up for it now,' she ventured, to be rewarded with a brief chuckle.

So gradually they settled into conversation again, but the former unselfconscious spontaneity was missing. Something had happened back there by the river and Robin was terribly afraid it was all down to that couple who had recognised him. Which seemed to suggest he was neither ready nor willing to have it known that he was taking an interest in her.

When they got back to Black Rock, he walked up to the

house with her. 'I'm afraid I can't ask you in for coffee,' she said as she fumbled in her bag for her key.

'Next time—when you're in your own place.'

'That's a promise.'

'Which I shall hold you to.' He put out his hands and drew her slowly towards him. 'Thanks for another lovely evening, Robin.'

'Just what I was about to say,' she breathed unsteadily. He was very close.

He kissed her with a hard and unexpected passion before striding away with a muttered goodnight. Robin stood with a hand over her clamouring heart and watched him out of sight.

It was fine next morning and Robin saw the bay all sparkling in the sun when she drew back her curtains. It was also later than she'd thought and Rory would soon be here, bringing Eorna to be looked after. Last night he had left her, if possible, even more confused than ever. He found her attractive—she was sure of that now—but was it solely on her own account or just because she reminded him of Deirdre? And how deep did it go? He'd not been pleased when those acquaintances came upon them last night, down by the river. Wisely Robin decided that only time would show the nature of his feelings—and her own. For how much of what she was feeling was a rebound reaction from David? Besides, there was the glamorous Selina.

When Rory's car stopped at the gate, Mrs McKenzie was the first to notice. 'If he is wanting you to work . . .' she began, but Robin called over her shoulder that she was only taking his dog for the day. That Mrs McKenzie found this highly significant Robin was in no doubt as she sped down the drive.

As usual, Eorna gave her a rapturous greeting and Rory told her she wasn't supposed to eat Robin, no matter how delicious she might be. To Robin he said, 'You know, you are remarkably kind to think of taking on this monster.'

'Not at all,' she denied, savouring the delicious bit. 'As I'm always telling you, I'm glad to oblige the boss. What time would you like her back?'

'It seems a cheek, but if you could keep her all day—I've a feeling it's going to be hectic.'

'Surely. Nineish, then?'

'Perfect. And if I'm in, which I hope I will be by then, I'll have the coffee-pot going. If I should be out, then just put her in the house. The back door is always unlocked.'

'I'll do that.' Robin took Eorna's leash from him. 'You'll be wanting to get started.'

He sighed. 'Yes, I suppose I'd better. There have been three calls already. Have a nice day, *caileags*.'

'We'll have a great time, won't we, Eorna? Don't work too hard.'

Nothing there to fuel the fires should Mrs McKenzie be curtain-twitching, thought Robin, as she put Eorna into her car.

Almost as soon as Rory drove away, clouds whipped up from the west and rain was soon falling steadily. From then on, the day deteriorated in all ways. The minute Calum arrived at Fratini's, it was obvious that he'd been crying and could start again at any moment. Robin lined up his usual quota and waited for him to tell her what was wrong in his own time.

He was into his third chocolate sundae before he felt strong enough. 'She's takin' me back, Robin. In the morn.' His lower lip was quivering, despite his manful attempts to stay calm.

'Your mother? To Glasgow?'

He nodded. 'She says she's missin' him. The auld fella. "Well, Ah'm no' ", Ah says. "So can I no' stay here?" '

' "Naw," she says. "Ye're needin' a faither's haund." '

His jaw jutted pugnaciously. 'If he leathers us like he used tae, Ah'll set the polis on him—Ah'm tellin' ye!'

'You do that. He mustn't beat you, darling.' Robin swallowed hard, feeling she might cry herself. 'Does he drink, your father?'

'Aye—and lays aboot him like a cuddy driver.' His face brightened. 'Mebbe she's forgot a' that. Mebbe we'll be comin' back, Robin.'

'Oh, I hope so, Calum. I shall miss you.'

'Me as well.' He looked like crying again so Robin said hastily, 'If this is our last day—for a while—then let's not waste it. Finish your ice and then we'll go to the Amusement Arcade until it stops raining.' She hated the place, all that noise and the flashing lights, but Calum adored it and he must have everything he wanted today.

About twelve, the sun peeped out for long enough to tempt them up on the hills, only to yield to rain again as soon as they were nicely distanced from the car. Eorna got soaked and Robin anxiously towelled her dry, only to have her escape at once and go chasing after grouse through the sodden heather.

'And you get ontae us for swearin',' reproved Calum, listening to Robin's muttered cursing.

Next time, there was only the car rug to dry her with, so the car reeked heavily of wet retriever all the way back to Bratanport and both Robin and Calum were glad to get out and go for a fish supper at Fratini's.

Calum was very quiet on the drive back to the cottage but even on his last day and in the pouring rain, he still refused to let her drive him right up to the cottage. He thrust a grubby piece of paper into her hand. 'Ma address, Robin. See an' write tae us now.' Then in an unexpected burst of sentiment he flung his arms round her neck and charged her never to forget him. Robin hugged the puny body and said no she wouldn't and yes she would write and he must write back, all the time wondering if he actually could. He was said to be away from the school more than he was in it.

'Aye—Ah wull.' Then he flung out of the car and fled up the path without looking back, as if pursued by fiends. Sadly Robin watched him go, feeling she was losing a true friend. Then she drove back to Black Rock to tidy herself up before returning Eorna to her master.

No Range Rover in the drive suggested that Rory was out, for he'd never bother to garage it when on call. So Robin towed a reluctant Eorna round to the back. The first thing she saw in the kitchen was Selina Stuart-Strang's beautiful Paisley shawl thrown carelessly over a chair.

So what? She was a friend of Rory's and a close friend at that. And if Robin was wise then she'd better not forget that. She rummaged in her bag for her engagement book and tore out a page to leave a note saying she hoped Eorna wouldn't suffer any ill effects from her soaking. Then, leaving the animal asleep in front of the Aga, she slipped quietly out.

Tomorrow being the thirty-first, she would be moving to the cottage, so Robin went straight to her room to pack. She was getting ready for bed when she was called down to the phone. It was Rory. 'I'm so sorry I missed you—I'd been looking forward to seeing you—but I was called over to Dunleathann and I've only just got back.'

'Nothing serious, I hope.'

'No—just indigestion due to a hefty snack of heavy ale and mussels. I ask you, what a combination for a ninety-year-old! Robin, thank you for looking after Eorna today. It was just as hectic as I feared. Was she a nuisance?'

'Oh, no.' May she be forgiven. 'I loved having her and so did Calum. Oh, Rory! His mother's taking him back to Glasgow tomorrow. And he told me his father gets drunk and beats him.'

'Don't worry, *caileag*. If we can screw an address out of the family, we'll get Strathclyde Social Services to keep an eye on him.'

'I've got it—he gave it to me.'

'Then we're half-way there.' A little pause and then he said, 'I'm so sorry we weren't able to spend some time together today.' He'd spent time with Selina, though! 'How about tomorrow?'

'Tomorrow,' said Robin, 'is moving day.'

She took a touching farewell of Mrs McKenzie and Flora after breakfast next morning, Mrs McKenzie repeating her strict injunctions about Robin remembering to feed herself properly.

By now, everybody in Vallersay knew that Robin was leaving Black Rock and going to live in one of Fergus McInnes's cottages at Braeheid Farm. Her patients had used this as an excuse to shower her with presents. There were so many that after lunch, Morag went and found a large cardboard box from the storeroom and they packed it together. 'Good lord, is it your birthday or what?' asked Rory when Robin cannoned into him as she carried it out to the car.

'Sorry, I couldn't see where I was going.'

'I'm not surprised.' He took the box out of her arms and carried it the rest of the way. 'It'll have to go on the front seat,' he said when he saw the car packed tight already. 'If you add this, you'll obscure your rear-view mirror.'

'Oh, dear, and I've still to pick up my grocery order from McKenzie's.'

'In that case . . .' He hoisted the box on to the back seat of his own car. 'I'll bring this up to you after evening surgery. Will that do?'

Not half it wouldn't! 'That's immensely kind of you.'

He smiled down at her. 'I am immensely kind—just like you.'

'In fact, we're both pretty marvellous,' she retorted, eyes dancing in response.

Morag stood by, watching and listening, wide-eyed and fascinated.

All the ward patients wanted to share in the excitement of the move and Robin was kept busy answering questions about the cottage in between treatments. Mrs Claddaich McKenzie in particular was much better that day. She was showing good recovery in her affected arm and even managed to walk a few steps without help.

After work, Robin collected her grocery order and drove up to Braeheid in a mood of happy expectancy. Fergus was hovering on the doorstep and insisted on carrying everything inside for her.

When Robin had first seen it, the cottage had been strewn with the possessions of the previous occupants. Now it was very tidy. She looked round, admiring the simple pine table and chairs, tapestry sofa, matching curtains and cottage-style armchairs. She remarked with pleasure on the bowl of roses on the long coffee-table.

'Just a small gesture of welcome,' said her landlord, looking pleased. 'I wish I could stay and help you settle in, but I've got my accounts to do for the end of the month.'

Robin assured him he'd been the greatest help already and had hardly shut the door behind him before Lindsay arrived, carrying a large covered tray which she dumped on the worktop in the kitchen. 'A quiche and a few other things for your supper,' she explained. 'I bet you never gave a thought to what you were going to eat tonight, and even if you did, you'll be much too excited to cook.' She gazed round and decided the place really was the palace Robin had said.

'I knew you'd like it, but wait till you've seen the rest.' Proudly Robin showed off her sage-green shower-room and neat wee bedrooms; one with bunks and the other with twin beds.

'I must remember to ask Fergus where he got those gorgeous duvet covers,' said Lindsay as they returned to the living-room. 'And talking of Fergus, that was him I saw leaving as I drove up, wasn't it?'

'It was. He came to say welcome and ended up carrying everything in for me.'

'Well, just so long as that was all he came for. He's good company but you'll need to watch him, Robin.'

'So people keep telling me, but I think I can cope.'

'Just see that you do.' Lindsay frowned at her watch. 'I'll be back one day soon for a real visit, hen, but right now I have to go home and feed my family of gannets.'

When she had gone, Robin spent half an hour or so unpacking and finding places for everything, then she went to the kitchen to put Lindsay's quiche in the oven. When Rory arrived, she was standing on the little terrace outside the living-room window, admiring her view.

Before she could go and let him in, he came round and they went in together through the patio door. He put the box on the table and sniffed appreciatively. 'Something smells good.'

'Thanks to Lindsay, I shall be eating well for days. Unless of course you'd like to stay and help me eat it.'

'I was terribly afraid you weren't going to ask,' he said. He reached into the present box and pulled out several bottles: sherry, some wine and several bottles of her favourite mineral water. 'Just a small moving-in present.'

'Oh, you are good. How lovely!' She poured him a glass of sherry, orange juice for herself and they went to sit on the couch. With the coffee-table in front of them half covered in roses, Rory could hardly fail to notice them.

'Yes, aren't they lovely? Courtesy of my kind landlord.'

'Is that a fact now?' He pulled a face. 'You want to watch him, remember.'

'So says everybody, but he seems harmless enough to me.'

'That,' said Rory significantly, 'is half the trouble.'

'I'll remember. More sherry?'

'And why not? I'm off duty tonight.'

After supper, they sat on the couch again and the space between them gradually disappeared as the evening wore on. After a lengthy and definitely delicious interlude, Rory said thoughtfully, 'This is getting to be quite a habit, isn't it?'

Robin settled her head more comfortably on his shoulder. 'Just what I was thinking.'

'Any objections?'

'Not so long as we keep it light.'

'And you think we are?'

'It was your idea,' she reminded him.

'Things—don't always follow the prescribed pattern.'

'I've noticed. All the same . . .'

'I've told you before about talking too much,' he said, taking her in his arms again. This time his kisses were urgent and demanding, and Robin was scared at the strength of the response he awakened in her. She wasn't nearly sure enough of herself, or of him, to let things rush along at this pace. With a great effort she freed herself and muttered, 'It's getting late.'

After a moment he asked softly, 'Does that mean you're sending me home?'

Nervously she picked imaginary bits of fluff off her skirt. 'Yes—it does. Do you . . . mind?'

'Naturally—but somehow I think I'd be sorrier if you let me stay,' he answered gently.

'Why?' Because then he'd feel trapped? She needed to

know. 'Rory . . .'

He stood up and reached down to pull her to her feet and they walked to the door with his arm around her waist. 'At risk of sounding repetitive, I have to thank you for yet another memorable evening,' he whispered.

'Think nothing of it,' she answered, striving for cool.

Rory kissed her lingeringly on the mouth. 'I hope you don't really mean that, because I'd like to think there'll be a lot of others.'

'That rather depends,' she parried. On what exactly it is you're expecting of me would have been the truthful answer if he'd asked her to expand on that. But he didn't. He just kissed her again, and went away.

CHAPTER EIGHT

ROBIN didn't sleep much; the first night in a strange bed, of course, and nothing whatever to do with Rory's visit. Consequently she was up early, but then spent much too long wondering over breakfast how Rory would behave the next time they met. This made her so late that she had to take the car to work.

Only Mr McPhail needed an early treatment today and his chest would have cleared up long since if only he didn't smoke, thought Robin, fighting her way through the acrid haze surrounding his bed. They had had to put him in a room by himself because of it. 'Have you always smoked this much?' she asked, coughing.

'Aye, aye—it iss so calming for my nerves,' he explained serenely, but anybody more tranquil than him it was difficult to imagine. And bless him, he is nearly ninety; so what? thought Robin before getting down to work.

Before leaving the hospital, she looked into the women's ward to bid them a good morning because they'd have been hurt if she hadn't. They wanted to be told how the move had gone and then it was off to the Centre, preparing as she went a convincing retort for Mrs Campbell in case she had something to say about Saturday night. Today, though, she only wanted to describe a new and very peculiar symptom, and Robin breathed more freely. Her impromptu camouflage must have been a success.

When Robin passed Rory's door on her way to coffee

127

later on, he called her in. 'Shut the door,' he said firmly.

'Oh, dear—what have I done now?' she asked, complying and pretending dismay.

'Nothing, just exercising discretion.' He came across and took her firmly by the shoulders. Then he kissed her.

'Phew!' she exclaimed as soon as she could. 'I didn't expect that—and in working hours too.' She had resolved on remaining as detached as possible until he showed signs of really wanting it otherwise. And on remembering Selina at all times—but difficult that, when he behaved like this.

He chuckled softly. 'I don't always call you into my room in order to give you a rocket, do I?'

'Oh, no—you just launch it anywhere. If I were to put down a plaque every place you'd told me off, the floor would be covered.'

He looked rather guilty. 'Was it as bad as that?'

'Not quite. Only joking.' She glanced at her watch. 'My next patient is due in about two minutes, Doctor sir.'

Ruefully he kissed the dimple in her cheek. 'That's the way it goes. What I meant to do, until I was distracted by your beauty, was to ask when I could see you again.'

'I'm free tonight,' she said a little more eagerly than was absolutely wise.

'And I've promised to take Selina sailing if it's fine,' he returned with a comical shrug. 'But I'll look in afterwards.'

Oh, he would, would he? 'Sorry, but I've just remembered something I promised to do for—somebody.'

Very feeble, so no surprise that he obviously didn't believe her. 'All right—then what about tomorrow? I'm on call, but we could always hope.'

The only thing Robin really felt like hoping for was that Selina would fall overboard that night, but with a lightness she was really proud of she said, 'Fine. Come up to the cottage for supper then—that's if you don't mind a threesome with Dougal.' Because she could play that game too—if she had to.

Rory scowled blackly. 'You're not still seeing him, are you?'

'I don't intend to drop my old friends any more than you do.' When he didn't immediately reply to that she asked, 'Shall I buy three steaks, then?'

'No, thank you—I don't care to be an afterthought,' he returned crushingly.

'Neither do I,' answered Robin pointedly, just as Morag looked in to say that Robin's next patient had arrived.

Being kept busy for the rest of the morning prevented Robin from brooding on that brief interlude in Rory's surgery, but the minute her last patient left her thoughts homed in on it again. She hadn't expected him to drop Selina just like that—but then neither had she expected him to be quite so blatant about continuing to see her. 'What's he trying to do?' she asked the empty treatment-room. 'Build himself a reputation like Fergus's?' But the only thing she felt she could be reasonably sure of was that he wasn't seriously interested in either of them.

Robin crossed over to her locker to rummage in her big shoulder bag for lunch. Damn! Spoiled by all those weeks of pampering at Black Rock, she had quite forgotten to bring anything. Never mind, according to Morag the baker's shop just down the road sold really scrummy filled rolls.

As she dashed along a loud hail from a passing motorist caused her to check just as a Land Rover drew into the kerb. 'Can I give you a lift, Robin?' asked Fergus McInnes eagerly.

'No, thanks, I'm only going as far as McKenzie's. I

forgot to make myself a sandwich this morning.'

'Somebody who works as hard as you do deserves something better than a sandwich for her lunch. How about a crab salad at the Smugglers'?'

'That sounds wonderful, but I'm afraid I must be at the hospital by half one.'

'It's barely twenty-to now, so you've loads of time. Come on, hop in.'

Well, why not? She was hungry, the food at the Smugglers' Rest was legendary and she could do with a bit of cheering up after that brush with Rory. 'Then thank you very much. That'd be super.'

And so it was. Fergus was a charming companion and his simple, uncomplicated admiration—whether too easily bestowed or not—was very good for a girl's ego. He remembered about the time, too, and it wasn't long after the half-hour when he left her at the front door of the hospital. Robin was still smiling with gratitude as she entered the hall.

Rory and Ella were there, talking. He broke off and looked pointedly at the clock before saying sardonically, 'Nice to see you.'

Robin coloured and Ella rushed in with, 'Stop it, Rory. Robin's never been late before, and anyway, I've never known anybody rush about the way she does.'

'Oh, I'm not denying she's a very fast worker,' he retorted, leaving Robin in no doubt that he'd seen her getting out of Fergus's vehicle. 'Versatile too,' he added.

If she'd lifted her chin any higher she'd have had to look down her nose at him. 'Thank you, Dr Rory,' she returned firmly, 'but I'm only trying to follow your example.' She smiled sweetly at a somewhat perplexed Ella and stalked on. That had been a pretty good exit line, she felt, snatching a quick backward glance and catching Rory's furious expression. She had scored a point, then. Great—except that wasn't what she wanted at all. She wanted them to stop quarrelling, become really good friends—and, maybe, even fall in love some day. Whereas everything pointed to him just wanting a little bit on the side. Well, he wasn't going to get it!

Fuelled by fury, Robin fairly threw herself into her work that afternoon, spurring her patients on to lengths that surprised them. 'I walked twice down the ward and nearly all by myself,' purred Mrs Claddaich McKenzie delightedly. 'Do you not think Dr Rory will be letting me home soon, *mo ghaoil*?'

Robin said she wouldn't be surprised at anything Dr Rory did, which patients and nurses alike took to be a compliment. Tired of listening to all the adulation that followed, Robin was actually glad to exchange the women's ward for Mr McPhail's smoke-filled little room.

Her anger abated somewhat when the heavens opened at seven-thirty, unleashing their watery contents on the bay and everything in it. She calculated that Rory and Selina should be well away from land by now.

All next day, Robin didn't see Rory once and went home to cook dinner for Dougal feeling rather depressed, though she would have died rather than admit the cause. However Dougal's house-warming present did a lot to restore her spirits. He unwrapped it and hung it over the fireplace while Robin was busy in the kitchen. Coming out with the vegetable dish, she caught sight of it and stopped dead.

This was no hasty photographic representation of a beauty spot like the paintings he did for the tourists, but a thing of mysterious charm and colour—the contents only hinted at. Yet Robin had no difficulty identifying the beach where they had played all those years ago—or seeing Dougal, his sister, hers and herself in the children trailing seaweed at the water's edge. It was so hauntingly beautiful that she felt the tears pricking her eyelids.

Dougal took the dish from her and put it on the table. 'I'm glad you like it, Rob,' he said, though she hadn't said a word.

'Oh, Dougal! I knew you were a good painter, but I never realised you were a great one.'

He slumped down in his seat at the table and let out a great guffaw. 'Now if only the critics would react like that, my fortune would be made.'

Throughout the meal, Robin's eyes were constantly drawn to her picture, and Dougal was delighted with her reaction. It wasn't until he had gone that she realised he had only drunk one sherry and a can of lager all evening. She must ask him up often. If she could manage to stop him spending every evening in the pub, she wouldn't have come to Vallersay for nothing.

Robin had just finished washing up and putting away the dishes when she heard a knock at the door. Her heart sank as she remembered all those warnings. Not Fergus capitalising on yesterday's lunch surely? She went into the little vestibule and called out warily, 'Who is it?'

'Us,' shouted Rory, as Eorna set up a joyous barking.

Robin opened the door. 'I thought you were Fergus,' she said.

'Were you expecting him, then?'

'Certainly not,' she answered crossly. 'But then I wasn't expecting you either.'

'Blame her,' he said, meaning his dog now energetically inspecting the living-room. 'We were out for a walk and she—just sort of led me here.'

'I see.'

'What you can't see is all my goose-pimples,' he retorted. 'It's quite cold out here, you know.'

'I suppose you'd better come in, then.'

'Thank you very much for the gracious invitation,' he said, coming in and shutting the door.

'Do you often visit women late at night?' asked Robin coolly, still smarting from yesterday's clashes.

'What a crude way of putting it. I told you—this was Eorna's idea.'

'So you did. How silly of me.'

'Damn you, Robin, I had it in mind to apologise,' he said with sudden heat, 'but if you're going to keep up this ice-maiden imitation, then I don't think I'll bother.'

She thawed enough to put the kettle on for coffee—an action Rory noted. He followed her into the tiny recessed kitchen, bringing with him the faint but unmistakable smell of the operating theatre. 'Have you changed your aftershave?' she asked, edging round him to get at the cups.

'Oh, very witty. As a matter of fact I've just been setting a rather nasty fracture of right radius and ulna for a tourist unwise enough to fall off a ridge on Ben Iolair. Otherwise I'd have been here earlier.'

So this visit had been all Eorna's idea, had it? 'I thought you didn't want to be an afterthought,' she couldn't resist saying. 'Or had you forgotten that Dougal was coming?'

'I'm only surprised he isn't still here, but I expect he had to go for his nightly fix at the Fisherman.'

Robin stifled the angry retort that flew to her lips, because that could very well be why he had left when he did. So much for her good influence! 'Did you say something about an apology?' she asked instead, giving him a tiny smile and a cup of coffee.

'You gave as good as you got as usual,' he growled, following her into the living-room. 'But all the same, perhaps I was a bit hard on you yesterday afternoon—

and in front of Matron too.'

What a gift for understatement; yet an olive branch was an olive branch. 'I think honours were even in that particular battle.' She hesitated. Yes, she would say it—she was heartily sick of being at odds with him. 'I . . . kind of expected things to be—be better after that night when we went to see Mrs McKenzie,' she ventured haltingly, 'yet we still manage to quarrel. I wonder why?'

Rory had been standing well away from her with his back to the fireplace and Dougal's picture. Now he joined her by the window. 'Habit perhaps—I don't honestly know. All I do know is I wish we didn't.' He put an arm round her shoulders, making her jump—both from the contact and the suddenness of the gesture. 'That evening was just about perfect, wasn't it? So why don't we go back to the Brown Trout and see if we can't get back on the tracks? What do you say?'

Don't forget Selina, said the voice of caution, but Robin switched off. When he was near her like this—almost pleading for reconciliation—what could she say but, 'Oh, Rory—yes, let's.'

But when it came to setting a date, it seemed as if it would be nearly a week before they could go. Surely it was further proof of his sincerity that he phoned Archie to change on-call duties, making tomorrow possible? 'He'll take evening surgery too, so we can leave early. You'll want to come home first and pretty yourself up, I suppose, so I'll pick you up here about half six.'

'I'm not to go in uniform then, this time?'

Rory smiled into her eyes. 'I think we can recreate the atmosphere without that, don't you? Especially if the otters are there.'

He came nearer still. He's going to kiss me, she realised, wanting him to, yet still unable quite to stifle those doubts about his motives. Then suddenly Eorna set up a frantic barking outside in the courtyard that soon had all the farm dogs clamouring as well. 'She must have gone out through the window and found a mouse or something,' supposed Robin with a tremulous little laugh.

'Her timing is abysmal—no matter what,' hissed Rory, plunging outside to call her to heel as the doors opened in all the other cottages in response to the pandemonium. It took him several minutes, but having captured his dog at last, he came back to Robin. There were quite a lot of people still in the courtyard, discussing the rumpus, so he said, 'It's late. I'd better go before I ruin your reputation—if I haven't already.' Then he kissed her once briefly on the lips and went.

Their paths didn't cross all morning and in the afternoon, just when it looked as if they might contrive to walk back to the Centre together, Sister Urquhart came running to say that the emergency appendix was threatening to sign himself out as his cruising friends were moving on, and would Rory please come and speak to him.

'Coming, Sister.' He spread out his hands in a droll Gallic gesture of futility, promised Robin he would surely see her later, and obeyed the call. Robin watched him go and went back alone to finish her day while looking forward to the evening.

When she was ready, Robin poured herself a glass of apple juice and wandered out on to her little terrace to drink it. From here the view was clear right down to the road and she would see Rory coming. It was just such another splendid evening as the last time they had gone to the Brown Trout. A good omen perhaps? As she sighted the familiar square shape in the distance, her pulse accelerated, but she hardly had time to call herself to order before she realised it wasn't Rory but Fergus in his old Land Rover. She went back inside. If he saw her, he would probably call in and she didn't want Rory to find him there. Nothing must spoil this evening.

Fergus called anyway. 'It's such a splendid night, I wondered if you'd like to go for a drive,' he said. 'We could catch a bite to eat somewhere along the way.'

'You're very kind,' Robin told him, 'but actually I'm already fixed up for the evening. I'm being collected any minute now.'

'Just my luck,' reckoned Fergus, sounding truly disappointed. 'Who's the lucky man? Anyone I know?'

He'd know anyway when he saw the car, but she temporised, 'There's no need for me to tell you, the local network will do it soon enough.'

'How true. Still, if he lets you down, just give me a buzz.' He ran a practised eye over her neat figure in the full-skirted dress of turquoise cotton. 'We can't have all that feminine appeal going to waste.' He continued to stand there admiring her and Robin was wondering how to break off this flattering but untimely meeting when her phone began to ring, providing the impetus needed to speed Fergus on his way. She shut the door with relief and ran to answer it.

'Robin?' It was Rory's voice and before he could add how sorry he was she had guessed more or less what was coming. 'It's the laird.'

'A surgical emergency,' she presumed on a small sigh.

'Well, no—but I am his regular doctor.'

So he was of half the island, but would he cancel an evening off for just anybody? 'It doesn't matter,' she said, determined to hide both disappointment and suspicion. 'There'll be other chances.'

'Hey, steady on and don't jump to conclusions. This only means I'll be a bit late, that's all. An hour at the most.'

'Oh,' she said, feeling much better at once. 'Shall I wait here or would you like me to drive down into the town?'

'Better wait at home and I'll be out as soon as I can. And Robin—I really am sorry about this.'

'Yes, of course,' she said warmly in response to his obvious regret. 'See you soon then.'

She dragged a chair over to the living-room window and sat down to wait where she could see him coming. She waited not one hour, but more than two, and Rory didn't come. Another half-hour and Robin was driving tight-lipped into Bratanport to buy fish and chips at Fratini's; anything was better than making your own supper when you'd thought you were being taken out. She was out perhaps fifteen minutes. Rory did not ring again.

The first person Robin saw at the hospital next morning was Selina Stuart-Strang. She was pacing the hall looking wild and haggard, and her clothes looked as if she'd slept in them. 'Ah!' she exclaimed when she saw Robin. 'And about time too. You're needed to treat my father. Now.'

Robin felt her hackles rising at the girl's peremptory tone, but she made herself answer politely, 'I was very sorry to hear he had been taken ill,' as she headed for the office.

'In the private ward, for heaven's sake,' screeched Selina.

Robin turned and faced her coolly. 'As I know nothing of his condition, you must understand that I have to talk to my colleagues first.'

Ella explained all about the laird's acute asthma attack. Fortunately Rory had arrived at the Big House just before he went into respiratory failure, but, fearing the worst if he had to make the long journey to the mainland by helicopter before he was stable, he had transferred him to their hospital instead. Now he was in the room from which Mr McPhail had been hastily transferred, it being the only one equipped to deal with a ventilator case. It still smelt faintly of smoke.

'Are you familiar with the little old-fashioned Bird?' asked Ella quietly before they approached the bedside.

'Yes, but only for nebulising—not as a ventilator. But I gather they are extremely effective for their size. Is his chest very moist?'

'Sticky, more like, and I don't envy you the job of clearing it. Will you need help, Robin?'

At St Crispin's the physios worked in pairs on the ventilator cases, but this was Vallersay. Robin said she'd have a go first and shout for help if necessary, as all the nurses would be busy at this time.

'Thanks, dear,' said Ella, relieved. 'I think you'll find everything you need on the trolley.'

They had never met before, but Robin sensed that the laird, although rendered speechless by the tube sticking out of his mouth, was a lot more reasonable than his highly strung daughter. Treatment over, he managed to signify gratitude with a flickering smile. Robin bent over him and said gently, 'I'm sorry to put you through all this, but it's vital to keep your chest clear, so I'm afraid I'll be back again in a couple of hours.'

The old man made a wry face and raised a shaky hand to pat her arm, signifying acceptance. Robin tidied the bed and made sure everything was in order, then left, intending to report to Ella, but she found Rory and Selina arguing in the hall.

'I will not go home,' she was saying mutinously, her face dark with displeasure.

'And I say you will—you're only in the way here and there's absolutely no need for you to stay. He's not in any danger now, but he does need quiet.' Hearing Robin's soft footfall, he swung round, his face lighting up. 'So you've seen him already. Thanks, Robin. So how is he now?'

Robin reported in medical jargon and Selina demanded irritably, 'Speak simple English, can't you? Or isn't the patient's daughter allowed to know how he is?'

'Treatment was successful and will be repeated at two-hourly intervals as long as necessary,' said Rory in his kind doctor's voice before Robin could answer.

'Huh! I thought you said he needed quiet,' retorted Selina.

Rory turned his back on her to say in a low voice to Robin, 'You'll be wanting to hurry back and get started on your outpatients now so I'll not delay you—but I'll see you later.'

'Yes, Doctor,' agreed Robin, for Selina's benefit. But she felt herself dismissed as she walked away.

Rory came into her room at the Centre about half an hour later. 'About last night,' he began, and Robin put a warning finger to her lips as she rose from the desk. She nodded towards the closed cubicle curtains, where Mrs Campbell would be listening avidly.

They went out into the corridor. 'When I phoned again, you'd gone out,' he said. 'I suppose you were angry at being left in the lurch like that.'

She certainly had been—then. Now her anger had subsided into resignation. 'No, just hungry. I went out to get something to eat.' If only she'd waited another fifteen minutes . . .

'Oh, Robin, I'm so sorry. It was to have been so special.'

Impossible to go on being resentful when he looked at her like that. 'It was unavoidable—I know that.'

He relaxed visibly. 'I'm on all weekend, but would Monday be any good?

'I think so—but who knows?' She gave him a wry little smile. 'There might be another emergency.'

'Fate couldn't be that unkind. Same place, same time, then,' he insisted. 'But I'll be sure to see you before then. All work and no play . . .' The treatment timer sounded off in the room behind them, so he left her with a brief salute.

See you before then, Rory had said, and Robin believed he meant it. But it was his weekend on, and she herself would probably be in and out of the hospital all the time as well.

And so it proved. She had to cancel her regular baby-sitting evening for Jock and Lindsay because of the laird's continuing need. It was when she was about to make yet another visit to him early on Saturday evening that Robin overheard Rory talking to Selina in the laird's little room. Nothing sinister about that; doctor and patient's daughter in consultation. But were they? 'You're not going to let me down tomorrow, are you, Rory?' Selina was pleading with unusual humility.

Hand outstretched to push open the door, Robin paused. 'Have I ever? But I am on duty, so you mustn't be upset if I'm called away,' answered Rory.

'I promise I won't be—just so long as you do come.' Then in a softer caressing tone she added, 'I just don't know what I'd do without you, Rory darling.'

After a little pause he said, 'And I dare say I'd have to find another irritation without you to drive me nuts.' This elicited a delighted chuckle from Selina and, heart thumping, Robin tip-toed away to get herself together out of earshot. There was no point any longer in trying to ignore the fact that Rory was playing a double game. She must watch her step if she was to keep her heart and her pride intact. Meanwhile, she had a very sick patient to treat. Stumping back down the hall as noisily as her rubber-soled shoes would allow, Robin hurrumphed loudly outside the door before knocking.

Rory opened it. 'Robin! Good to see you. I've kept on just missing you all day.' He asked Selina to wait outside, then gave Robin a quick run-down on the laird's condition. She thanked him in her best professional manner before turning her attention to her patient. He needed a longer treatment than usual, and Robin took her time about changing out of uniform in Ella's office, but Rory was waiting by her car when she went outside. He was alone.

'Where's Selina?' she asked in surprise.

'I managed to persuade her to go home. She's been almost living here since Thursday and she's absolutely worn out.'

I've been here quite a lot myself, thought Robin, irritated by his obvious concern for the spoiled girl.

Almost as if he'd read her thoughts he went on, 'And you must be worn out too. These sole charge posts are hell at times like this. Come on up to the house and I'll rustle us up some supper.'

If Fergus really is one for the girls, then I think I can guess who taught him, Robin found herself thinking, but she'd better not give herself away or Rory would guess she had overheard his conversation with Selina. 'Thank you, I wish I could,' she made herself say brightly, 'but unfortunately I've got a prior engagement.'

'Oh, have you?' he observed, frowning.

Before he could ask for details she rushed on, 'Yes, and if I don't hurry, I'll not fit it in before I'm due back to treat the laird again. And that would never do, would it?' She got into her car and shot away with a scattering of gravel and what she hoped was a carefree wave through the open window. When she rounded the bend in the drive, a glance in her rear-view mirror showed Rory still staring after her.

'I thought you'd ditched me in favour of the boss again,' said Dougal humorously when Robin joined him at the Smugglers' later than she'd said she would.

'No way,' she denied decisively, squeezing in beside him. The place was packed tonight and it was a miracle he'd managed to keep her a seat at all.

'That was a short truce,' he observed. 'What went wrong?'

They were now once again the firm friends they'd been as children and Robin didn't hesitate to tell him how Rory was seeing her and Selina more or less on alternate nights.

Dougal whistled. 'I have to admire both his taste and his skill—not to mention his good fortune,' was his first reaction, which was absolutely no comfort at all. 'But cheer up, Rob. No man in his senses could prefer her to you for long. The usual?'

Robin almost said no, tonight she'd have a large gin and tonic and to hell with the consequences, when she remembered that work wasn't over for the day. So she nodded and said, 'Please.'

Dougal lounged over to the bar to get her drink, and when he came back with it he asked if she'd like to hear some good news. 'It would make a nice change,' Robin decided wryly.

'I didn't tell you, because frankly I didn't think I had a hope, but I sent a couple of my real paintings to the Royal Scottish Academy's summer exhibition. It seems they've made quite a stir and the upshot is—they're putting on a special show of my stuff during the Festival.'

'Oh, Dougal—that's marvellous!' It was too, and

enough to push her own problems aside for the moment.

'I knew you'd be pleased. The thing is, Rob, I'd like to include your picture if you don't mind.'

'Mind? I'd be honoured. "Loaned by Miss Robin Maxwell MCSP" would look splendid in the catalogue.'

'Philistine,' he teased. 'I don't believe you'd know a decent landscape from an advert for fertiliser!'

Robin promptly rose to that provocation, but her riposte was interrupted by some people coming up to congratulate Dougal on his sudden fame.

'Wonderful how a ne'-er-do-well suddenly becomes respectable and popular the minute he makes good, isn't it?' remarked Dougal after they had gone. 'You wait—it's only a question of time until I'm asked to dine at the Big House.'

This immediately brought Selina to mind—and her sick father who was almost due for his last treatment of the day. Another band of well-wishers had collected round Dougal by the time she left, including some who came through from the restaurant on hearing Dougal was in the hotel. But Dougal was shrewd. No amount of lionising would turn his head. He'd made that clear with his penetrating remark about success and popularity going together. What a pity she couldn't show a similar shrewdness in her own life, thought Robin as she drove back to the hospital.

Coming out again, after treating the laird who had seemed a little better, Robin couldn't stop herself glancing at Rory's house as she passed. It was in darkness. But was that because he was out on a call—or up at the Big House, comforting Selina?

The next day was Sunday—Robin's first in Vallersay without Calum. But since the day was dominated by the laird's need for frequent treatment, Robin didn't miss him quite as much as she'd expected. There was the occasional lull though and then she caught up with her correspondence, including a long letter to Calum, and then, towards teatime, she decided to go home for a reviving shower and a change of clothes on this close and sticky day.

Fergus must have been on the look-out, because he was pounding on the door before she could carry out her plan. 'It occurred to me,' he said when she opened up, 'that a hardworking lass like you might not have time to prepare a meal, so how about coming up to the house for supper later? Just tell me when it would suit and I'll have it all ready for you.'

If rumour was to be believed, then falling in with that would be tantamount to sticking her head in the lion's mouth, so Robin thanked him kindly and said firmly that she'd not have time in between her hospital duties.

'But you've still got to eat,' he persisted, 'so why don't I come down to the town and take you to the Royal Stuart?'

He seemed so determined that it was going to be very difficult to refuse. I'll be driving myself, she thought, and he can't do me much harm in a crowded restaurant. Most of all, there would be some satisfaction to be got from going out with another man while Rory danced attendance on Selina. 'I'd like that, thank you,' she said, and Fergus went away looking complacent.

Knowing their time was limited, Fergus had ordered their meal to be served the instant Robin appeared in the dining-room. This was the first time she'd been in Bratanport's premier hotel and she recognised several of Vallersay's foremost inhabitants in among the well-heeled holiday visitors. Fergus was an entertaining and thoughtful host, and Robin enjoyed his company as much as the excellent meal. And it was undeniably restful to be with a man who was so likeable, yet who didn't attract her.

Looking round on leaving, she spotted Netta and Archie dining with the couple she and Rory had met the previous Saturday at Bracken Lodge. She smiled and waved, not sure whether they saw her or not. But better that than having them think she didn't want to be seen.

'You've gone all quiet on me,' reproved Fergus, slipping an arm round her waist as they walked to her car.

'Have I? Then I'm sorry, but I can't help wondering how I shall find my patient when I get back to him.' Because you never did quite forget them, no matter what you were doing, when they were as ill as he was.

'Such dedication—you really are one of the most marvellous girls I've ever met,' maintained Fergus, staring into her eyes as his hand somehow slipped from waist to hip level. Feeling the suggestive pressure, Robin stiffened and side-stepped smartly. 'I bet you say that to all the girls,' she said, diving with relief into her little car. 'Thank you very much for my lovely meal—it was terribly kind of you,' she called as she drove away.

Phew! There had been a gleam in his eye which had borne out all she'd heard about him, so that had better be the last time she went anywhere with him. Life was quite difficult enough already.

CHAPTER NINE

IT HAD seemed to Robin on Sunday night that the laird was slightly improved, so it was very depressing to be met by a grim-faced Ella next morning, and to hear that he was developing a chest infection. Far from being able to scale down treatment, it could well become a twenty-four-hour job.

The same thought had occurred to Matron. 'In which case, you had better sleep here,' she decided. 'You can have my spare room and welcome.'

That would certainly be less tiring than to-ing and fro-ing from the cottage, and Robin thanked her warmly. She'd never imagined herself involved in intensive care when she decided to come to Vallersay—but then nothing about Vallersay had turned out the way she had expected.

She had just finished treating Mr Stuart-Strang when Rory and Archie arrived to check him over. As an anaesthetist, Archie was closely involved because of the ventilator. Afterwards, they all went to Ella's office for a discussion. A plan made for managing the laird's relapse, Robin would have left along with the others, but Rory called her back. 'You must be wondering how you're going to cope, Robin.'

'Ella and I have already considered that, and I'm going to sleep in her spare room until the crisis is over.'

'Very sensible, but help is at hand. I was at a dinner party last night.'

'Oh, yes,' she said, wondering how that was supposed

to help. At least he hadn't spent the whole evening alone with Selina!

'And at it, I discovered, among other things, that the wife of the new dentist is a physio.'

'Oh, yes,' repeated Robin with rather more interest.

'Yes, I thought that would intrigue you. She lost no time telling me how keen she is to work, so I'll get on to the Health Board offices as soon as I think they'll be awake and suggest we take her up on it. There's no way you can work round the clock without ending up as a casualty yourself.'

'They'll tell you they can't possibly afford it,' predicted Robin.

'If they'll not pay Mrs Crawford to help you, then I'll damn well pay her myself,' returned Rory grimly. 'You're looking quite washed-out enough already. I've asked her to come and discuss things with us tomorrow morning.' He sighed heavily. 'Having to put the old boy on two-hourly physio puts paid to our evening at the Brown Trout, I'm thinking.'

'Yes, it does, doesn't it?' Amazing that she should almost have forgotten about that, having been so thrilled when he arranged it. Yet maybe not. She'd overheard that revealing exchange between him and Selina since then.

'Is there anything wrong, Robin—apart from your being tired, that is?' he sounded so concerned that Robin wondered if she could possibly be misreading the Selina situation.

'No, nothing,' she answered, managing a smile. 'Why?'

He came nearer. 'It would have been nice if you'd said you were disappointed about tonight.'

'Oh, I am,' she returned quickly, her doubts dissolving as they always did when he was with her—in spite of what she thought he was up to when he wasn't.

'I hope so.' He laid a gentle hand on her shoulder. 'I shall make it up to you with interest once this crisis is over. Meanwhile, come up to the house between your evening treatments tonight. It's gey handy for the hospital and I'll do the best I can about some supper, though heaven knows I'm no cook.'

'Then let me see to it,' she offered promptly, capitulation complete. What had happened to the level-headed girl she used to think herself?

Both hands on her shoulders now, Rory rocked her gently, playfully. 'Idiot! You're missing the point completely. Don't you realise I'm trying to look after you?'

'That,' she said wryly, 'is not something I'm very used to.'

'Then it's high time you were.' He dropped a light kiss on the end of her nose. 'Report to me at seven-thirty sharp, Miss Maxwell.'

'Yessir—certainly, sir,' she responded, totally happy now.

'That's better, I like a bit of discipline in the ranks,' he said with an approving chuckle. 'Now we'd better get some work done, don't you think?'

St Crispin's Law, which stated the busier you were, the busier you got, prevailed in Vallersay too, and Robin acquired no less than five new patients that day. However, she did manage half an hour at home for a shower and a change of clothes before reporting as ordered at Rory's house.

The minute he opened the door to her, Robin realised that he had something on his mind. He regarded her sombrely for a second too long before saying, 'Well, come in, then—it's all ready,' in a rather cheerless voice.

'Thank you,' seemed the only thing to be said in return. Even Eorna wasn't as boisterous as usual. In tune with her master's mood, perhaps?

Rory led the way to the kitchen. 'I don't bother with the dining-room—too much trouble. I hope you don't mind.'

'No, of course not. Anyway, I always feel it's a compliment to be entertained in the kitchen.'

He gave her a look which suggested no compliment had been intended. 'Can I help at all?' she asked, her eager anticipation rapidly evaporating. Whatever was wrong? When she'd left the laird less than an hour ago he had been about the same, but in case he was what Rory was worrying about she said, 'I've tried to be careful about cross-infection, but perhaps with treating other chest patients I might have carried something to Mr Stuart-Strang.'

'Good God, nobody's blaming you for that,' he said brusquely. 'These things happen and it's rarely anybody's fault. Sit down.' He slapped a grilled steak down on the table in front of her and pushed across a tastefully arranged dish of vegetables.

'I thought you said you couldn't cook,' she said. 'This looks absolutely delicious.'

Rory shrugged. 'I have to confess that Netta did most of it. She—just happened to call at the right time.' He laughed mirthlessly, but Robin couldn't see what was so funny.

'It must be nice to have a cousin so near.'

'Yes, Netta has my interests very much at heart,' he stressed, sending her a look that was obviously intended to convey something, though she couldn't think what.

'That's—nice,' she observed, now feeling definitely uneasy.

Except for occasional remarks exchanged with exaggerated courtesy, the meal was eaten in near silence. By the time they carried their coffee into the sitting-room, the atmosphere was electric and Robin decided suddenly that she couldn't take any more of it. When Rory went to stand looking moodily out of the window, she followed him. 'I think you've got something fairly weighty on your mind,' she said with a nervous little giggle.

He glanced down at her, his face dark. 'You noticed.'

'I could hardly help it—and you were in such a good mood this morning.'

'That was this morning. I've learned a thing or two since then.'

Which left her no wiser. 'Is it—anything I could—help with? But perhaps you'd rather not talk about it,' she added hastily, watching his frown intensifying.

'Why not? I've got nothing to hide. Why did you ignore my warning about Fergus McInnes?'

'Well, I'll be . . .' Robin sat down heavily on the window-seat. That she had not been expecting—she had actually begun to wonder if Selina had told him it was time to send her packing! She collected her wits. 'I didn't—but he is my landlord. So—I try to be polite to him.'

'And your idea of being polite is to let him flaunt you all over Bratanport at expensive restaurants, is it?'

Netta, of course. She had seen her with Fergus last night and that was why she had just happened to call. 'He has taken me out for a couple of meals on the spur of the moment, yes. I thought it was rather kind of him.'

'You're either very naïve or very stupid,' he returned coldly. 'Remember this is Vallersay where nothing goes

unnoticed. And don't forget you've also been seen
about with me. What do you suppose people are making
of that?'

Robin leapt to her feet as if stung. Now she knew
what was upsetting him. His pride was dented. Well,
what of hers? 'Not a lot, they must be too confused,'
she returned deliberately. 'Because you are also seen
about a whole lot more with Selina Stuart-Strang!'

'That is entirely different,' he retorted loftily.

'Why? Because it happens to suit you? But if I do
exactly the same thing, that's taboo. How come?'

'There is absolutely no parallel!' he thundered.

Of all the nerve! 'Of course there is!' she yelled back.
'And only a . . . a chauvinistic dog-in-the-manger would
say otherwise!'

'I knew it was a mistake to let this thing go beyond the
professional,' he roared.

'I couldn't agree more,' she screeched, 'so that's the
way we'll keep it in future. And now it's time for me to
be professional and go and treat your dear friend
Selina's father.' She went—and Rory was either too
astonished, or too furious, to stop her.

Naturally Robin was too occupied to give a thought
to the quarrel during the laird's treatment session;
likewise during the cosy chat over a cup of tea with Ella
in her tiny sitting-room. But once bedded down in Ella's
spare room, Robin could no longer keep from thinking.
However had it happened at all? She had no intention of
going out with Fergus again, so why couldn't she have
told Rory so? Yet how could she, when it had been so
obvious that his main concern was his public image?
And the way he had refused to discuss Selina was very
significant. It suggested she was on a higher plane
altogether—and therefore sacrosanct. Clearly he had no
intention of giving her up—and you've had quite

enough of playing second fiddle in your life, Robin lectured herself. Result? *Impasse*. So, since it had to end some time, better now before you get too fond of him.

Add all that trauma to three visits to Selina's father during the night, and it was no wonder Ella said that Robin was looking completely washed out when she brought her breakfast in bed next morning.

'You shouldn't be doing this,' said Robin, attempting to open her eyes more than half-way as she heaved herself up into a sitting position.

'Nonsense! I do this for my visitors—it keeps them out of my road. And talking of visitors, when is it your parents are coming, Robin?'

'By the last boat on Friday, and they'll stay a fortnight, I hope. They love Vallersay and will find lots to do while I'm working.'

'Let's hope things have calmed down a bit by then or they'll take one look at that white face of yours and whisk you off home with them.' Ella's parents must have been the sort who went on organising their daughters' lives right up to the altar and beyond, surmised Robin as the door closed behind Matron's ample form.

All the same, she does have a point, she thought a little later, wrinking her nose distastefully at her reflection in the bathroom mirror. Being of a romantic disposition, her mother would be sure to suppose her daughter to be pining for David, whom she had approved of, calling him the strong, silent type. What a laugh—when he was in fact a rotten conversationalist and turned out to be weaker than water. Robin froze in the act of brushing her teeth. If she could think that, then the Vallersay cure had worked. But had she merely exchanged one unsatisfactory relationship for another even more—upsetting?

There was no change in Mr Stuart-Strang's condition,

and after leaving a short written report for the doctors—being on the spot, Robin was earlier than usual and would miss them—she went down to the Centre to get ready for her outpatients, mindful of the necessity to find time to talk to Mrs Crawford later on.

Rory brought the dentist's wife to Robin's room himself. Having introduced them, he said to the newcomer, 'Miss Maxwell will put you in the picture far better than I could, but if you have any queries afterwards I shall be here until twelve.' He didn't address Robin directly at all.

'What a charming and helpful man,' admired Mrs Crawford when he had gone.

'That is the general view,' agreed Robin quietly. 'Now what would you like me to tell you about first?'

'The ventilator patient who seems to be causing such a stir,' was the prompt response.

The knowledgeable way she reacted and the searching questions she put soon convinced Robin of her high calibre, and it was no surprise to learn that Anne Crawford had been lecturing for several years. 'I gather I only missed the chance of applying for your job by a few weeks,' she said later as they walked up to the hospital to see the laird. 'So if you ever think of leaving, please tell me at once. I need something to do now that both our children are away at college and this job would be ideal.' She eyed Robin curiously. 'I'm from Islay myself, and as an islander I must confess I'm very curious to know what brought you to Vallersay.'

'I've always loved the place and I've got friends here,' returned Robin casually, before introducing Anne to the laird.

It was soon obvious that Anne wasn't just an academic, but a skilful practitioner as well. Had she been free to apply when she herself had, Robin knew there would have been no contest. She wouldn't have come to Vallersay, wouldn't have met Rory and wouldn't have . . .

'. . . suits you, and Dr McEwan, of course, I would suggest that I take on Mr Stuart-Strang's treatment on alternate nights,' Anne Crawford was saying in the way of one whose suggestions are seldom ignored. 'I'm afraid I can't manage more at the moment, with half our chattels still in crates.'

'Any help you can give me will be much appreciated,' agreed Robin, having collected her thoughts.

They parted on the hospital steps, with Robin promising to confirm the arrangement after she had spoken to Rory. He was out when Robin got back to the Centre. It was raining heavily by then, so she and Morag had their lunch in the little kitchen where Rory found them some time later. He refused Morag's offer to make him coffee with one of his famous smiles, then asked Robin in a markedly cooler way what she had arranged with Mrs Crawford. 'And does that satisfy you?' he asked when she had told him.

'Oh, yes. I'll be more than grateful just to be able to sleep peacefully every other night.'

'What it is to have a clear conscience,' he observed with unmistakable irony, provokingly departing before Robin could think of a suitable reply.

'I am just thinking what a terrible tease our Dr Rory is,' breathed Morag, blissfully unaware of any undercurrents.

Robin couldn't think of a fitting reply to that, either—or rather, none that Morag would approve. 'He is certainly . . . unusual,' she allowed as they both went back to work.

It was good to hand over to Anne Crawford at six and know she was definitely off duty until eight next morning. The only snag was returning to the cottage—altogether too conveniently placed for any unwelcome attentions Fergus might decide to bestow. Still, if she could keep him at bay until the weekend she would have her parents as chaperons and, by the time they went, surely a man of Fergus's extreme susceptibility would have found another attraction?

The week wore on. The laird gradually improved and several ward patients were discharged, including Mrs Claddaich McKenzie who went home on Friday, loud in praise of Robin's skill. 'Just think—all this in less than three weeks,' she kept saying. Was it really so short a time since that halcyon evening with Rory?

In Outpatients, Rory summarily discharged Mrs Campbell when she told him that this time—if anything—the treatment was making her worse. 'Did you ever hear the like?' she demanded of Robin. 'And me in my state of health. I think I will be changing my doctor.'

Robin had hardly seen Rory all week, all necessary messages being passed through a third party. Impossible not to realise he was deliberately keeping out of her way, as never before. She missed him, and almost preferred their early sparring days to this. So, his present attitude being what it was, Robin was very surprised to be summoned to Rory's consulting room late on Friday afternoon. He was dictating a report and kept her waiting until he had finished it. That done, he said at last, 'I've got Mr Stuart-Strang's latest X-ray here. Come and look at it.'

Obediently Robin followed him to the viewing screen in the corner. He was being very careful that their bodies shouldn't touch, but she was still acutely aware of his nearness. She jumped, startling them both when he demanded abruptly, 'Well? What do you think?'

'It's almost normal,' she stammered, collecting her scattered wits.

'Is it?'

'Well—the diaphragm is perhaps still a trifle high on the left, but the secretions are all upper respiratory now.'

'Well observed,' he allowed judicially, turning off the viewing screen and swinging round to perch on the corner of his desk. 'Now he's off the ventilator we can cut physio to thrice daily.' He paused. 'I have persuaded Mrs Crawford to work tomorrow and Sunday.'

'You mean—I've got the whole weekend off?' Robin could hardly believe it.

'You have. You need the break and, with an eye to the future, Mrs Crawford was only too glad to oblige.'

When she heard the word future, Robin felt an ominous coldness in the pit of her stomach. 'I'm not sure I understand,' she said unsteadily, only too afraid that she did.

'Oh, come now,' he said with a trace of his old impatience. 'We both know you'll not be staying here for ever.'

At his scathing tone, apprehension transmuted to anger. 'Great! Just let me know when you want me to hand in my notice, won't you?'

'There's no need for histrionics,' he returned coolly, 'but facts are facts—and I would have thought that a girl of your professionalism would be glad to know that when she does go, she'll not be leaving patients and colleagues in the lurch.'

In short, now that Anne Crawford was here, she could take herself off any time she liked. Stifling another angry retort, Robin went for dignity this time. 'I am very grateful to you for arranging my weekend off. And as for the rest—it's just as well to know where

I stand. May I go now, please?'

Rory had been watching her intently ever since he
raised the possibility of her departure. Now a tiny spasm
of emotion distorted his face for one brief second. 'Why
not?' he asked woodenly. 'It's well after hours. Have a
nice weekend.'

Robin set off to meet her parents off the boat in a
decidedly gloomy frame of mind. Until today, she had
had at the back of her mind the idea that some time,
somehow, she and Rory would settle their quarrel. Now
she was forced to admit that a Hebridean drought was a
likelier prospect. To her horror, she felt hot tears
pricking her eyelids. Worse and worse! Far from
learning from past mistakes, she seemed to have
repeated them. 'My next job had better be in a convent
or a girls' school,' she muttered bitterly, as she parked
by the harbour wall and got out to lean on the wall and
watch the ferry grow from a small speck on the horizon
to something capable of carrying eighty cars.

Her parents' car was one of the first off the ferry, and
Robin ran to it as soon as they spotted her and slowed
down. Though warm, their exchange of greetings had to
be brief because of the congestion on the pier.
Promising them a proper welcome at the cottage, Robin
returned to her own wee Jap and led the way. As she
had expected, they were very taken with her new home.
'Quite comfortable enough to be lived in all year round.
Except that . . .' her mother paused, looking sly.

When her mother didn't finish her sentence, Robin
said, 'It's long past your usual dinnertime, so you must
both be hungry,' and went across to the kitchen to check
that all was well in the oven. She's going to tackle me
about David, she thought. Well, anything was better
than having her mother get an inkling of her present
emotional mess!

Drinks poured—sherry for her mother, a dram of his favourite malt for her father and orange juice for herself—Robin proposed a toast to Vallersay.

'To Vallersay,' they echoed, going on to say how much they were looking forward to this holiday after so many years.

Then Mr Maxwell pointed his glass towards Dougal's picture and said, 'Your landlord must be a very trusting man to leave a painting of that quality in a rented place.'

'Ah, but that is mine,' Robin explained proudly, telling them all about Dougal and his recent success. Having exclaimed some more over that, they wanted to know when they would see him.

'Tomorrow night. I've asked everybody I know to come for cheese and wine so that you can meet them.'

This news immediately set her mother planning a full-scale feast, despite Robin's protestations. 'Save your breath,' advised her father. 'She'll get her own way in the end. She always does.' Robin left them laughingly disputing that while she went to dish up.

Supper over, Mr Maxwell refused coffee, saying it tended to keep him awake at nights now and if nobody minded, he thought he would have an early night.

'What a good idea,' applauded his wife. 'Then you'll be fresh for the party.' Having seen him tucked up with his usual glass of hot milk, Mrs Maxwell came back, eyes alight at the thought of what she would be telling her daughter as they washed the dishes.

Robin held her off for a minute by demanding a full report on her father's health but having given it, Mrs Maxwell announced importantly, 'I have had a letter from David.'

'David who?' Robin asked calmly as she ran hot water into the sink.

'There's no need to be coy, Robin. Your ex-fiancé, of course.'

'I wasn't being coy, Mother. It just never occurred to me that he would ever have written to you. What on earth did he want?'

'What he wants,' Mrs Maxwell paused dramatically, 'What he wants, Robin, is a reconciliation. He realises what a terrible mistake he made, and now he wants to make it up. Only before approaching you, he decided to contact me first to find out how you would react.'

Still the same old David, thought Robin dispassionately. Never one to risk an unnecessary blow to his pride. 'And where has Marcia gone swanning off to this time?' she wondered aloud.

'Darling, don't be so cynical—it worries me when you talk like that. The Marcia business is over. It's you he really loves, Robin, and he knows that now,' said Robin's mother in the thrilling accents of a soap opera matriarch.

'If I hadn't heard it all before, I might be more inclined to believe that, but in any case it's too late, Mother dear. I'm over him this time—I really am.'

'That's hurt pride speaking,' said Mrs Maxwell with a misplaced confidence that was rather galling. 'You'll see things quite differently when you've had time to think.'

'Perhaps.' Robin knew fine that she wouldn't but she wasn't going to start the holiday by arguing with her mother. Instead she changed the subject. 'This dish will need to soak overnight, so that's the lot, thank you, Mother dear. How about taking our coffee outside on my little terrace if the midges aren't out?'

Robin's father hadn't been wrong when he said that her mother always got her own way. In vain did Robin point out that she hadn't got either the plates or the cutlery to give her guests a full-scale supper. Mrs

Maxwell said confidently that she was sure that nice-sounding landlord of Robin's would be delighted to help them out.

And next morning, she had Robin down to Bratanport and waiting on the doorstep for McKenzie's stores to open. Their purchases occasioned much interest. 'Twenty-two pounds ninety-four, please, madam,' said Mrs Seonaid McKenzie, currently an outpatient of Robin's. 'You will be having a party, I am thinking, *mo ghaoil.*' Robin just had time to admit as much before her mother dragged her away to the baker's.

Back at the cottage, they worked non-stop all day and the result was a triumph. Dougal came first, looking almost conventional in a respectable, if dated, suit and with his hair and beard neatly trimmed. 'In keeping with my new image as a successful man,' he explained, amused at Robin's obvious surprise.

Lindsay, Jock and their children were next, and Lindsay's eyes widened when she saw the supper table. 'If I had only known you could turn out this sort of thing, Robin Maxwell, I'd never have had the nerve to feed you in my house,' she said forthrightly.

'This lot is all down to my mother. She's the one with the fancy diplomas,' confessed Robin.

'Well she's a wizard and no mistake.' Lindsay grabbed her youngest boy's hand a micro-second before it closed on the meringue he'd been coveting and then she led him away from temptation, just as the McLeods and the Drummonds came, bringing Morag with them. Close on their heels came Ella with Sister Urquhart and her husband. Nearly everybody here then. Robin busied herself with introductions, then helped her father to dispense drinks while trying hard not to keep glancing out of the big window with its uninterrupted view of the road.

She had deliberately chosen today for her party, knowing that Rory would be on call. He had to be asked along with the others, but she wanted him to have a cast-iron excuse for refusing—if that was what he wanted. And to show how forgiving and generous she was, she had included Selina in the politely worded little note she had left on his desk. His equally formal reply had declined for Selina, while leaving his own intentions provokingly unclear.

When the doorbell rang, her pulse rose to critical, but it was only Fergus. By now the big raftered living-room was echoing with the noise of laughter and chat. Mrs Maxwell had discovered that Hamish McLeod had once worked with her brother, now a GP in Perthshire, Robin's father was talking income tax with Archie, and Dougal was the centre of an admiring little group, headed by Ella.

'Your party is a howling success and no pun intended,' shouted Fergus in Robin's ear, seizing the chance to get his arm firmly round her waist at the same time. She hadn't managed to free herself when Rory walked in through the open window, just as he had at the Andersons' house on her very first day in Vallersay.

'Thanks—and I'm sorry my arrival was so inopportune,' he said acidly, having watched her free herself hastily before bringing him a drink.

'Not at all,' she denied firmly, fuming inwardly at being wrong-footed again. 'It is very good of you to come at all, when you're so busy.'

'Actually I'm not, or I wouldn't be here.'

'Oh, suit yourself. I was only trying to be polite.'

'Then perhaps you'd be best not to bother if it's such a strain.'

Robin longed to shake him. 'Here comes my mother,'

she hissed. 'So please try to be pleasant for once.'

'I know how to behave,' he hissed back, his expression changing miraculously to one of warmth and charm as Mrs Maxwell arrived beside them.

Robin left them as soon as she could, wandering disconsolately from group to happy group, topping up glasses and offering crisps and other titbits. But always she was aware of Rory, chatting first to her mother, then talking with her father. She hadn't expected him to spend so much time with them. Once she caught his eye and he sent her an 'I told you' so look. So he was only doing it to pay her out for telling him to try and be pleasant. Now they would be wondering why she'd disliked him so much and she might have a bad time explaining that. I wish he hadn't come, she thought. I wish I'd never thought of giving this stupid party. All I need now is to overhear my mother telling him that my ex-fiancé is back on the scene and my day will be complete.

Next minute, Robin spotted her mother in earnest conversation with Netta and knew she was under discussion by the way they both kept glancing her way. Heavens, telling Netta would be just as bad! Robin rushed over to break that up, praying she had been in time.

Soon after that, Mrs Maxwell decided it was time to eat, and, having made sure that everybody was served, nobody was temporarily alone and that her mother and Netta were now at opposite ends of the room, Robin slipped outside into the gathering dusk. A wide shaft of light from the window flooded the little terrace and she moved to the side to lean against the wall, in shadow. She stared down over Bratanport, by night a thick horseshoe of twinkling lights encircling the calm waters of the bay. Go away if you must, her friends had said

when she and David broke up. But why a remote
Scottish island? Why not somewhere exciting? Robin all
but laughed aloud at the memory. She'd had all the
excitement she could handle in Vallersay. But now it
was over—and only more heartache lay ahead.

Roused by footsteps on the cobbles at the side of the
house, she peered fearfully round the corner. Relieved,
she said foolishly, 'I thought you were Fergus,' when
Rory materialised at her side.

'I am sorry to disappoint you,' he returned coldly,
'but it would be neither polite—nor pleasant—to go
away without thanking my hostess for a delightful
party.'

'You—weren't here very long.'

'I am on call, as you must have known when you
fixed the date.'

'I didn't think you would—want to come.'

'Not to have put in an appearance would have been
noticed—and wondered about.'

'Of course. How silly of me not to think of that.'

'Perhaps it takes an islander to remember.' But for
somebody about to leave, Rory seemed in no hurry. He
too leaned against the corner of the house, though she
was standing on the terrace. So their shoulders were
level, and touching.

All Robin's powers of sensation seemed concentrated
in that few square inches of bare skin in contact with
Rory's sleeve. Just two thin layers of fabric between
them; his jacket and his shirt—both doing nothing at all
to diminish the feel of the hard muscle underneath. The
slightest movement of his and the consequent ripple sent
tiny frissons scurrying hither and thither—delicious,
and frustrating. Her fingers curled tightly, the nails
cutting into her palms as she fought the impulse to
throw herself against him and beg for forgiveness. It

no longer mattered that she was not solely to blame. Only the fear that he would repulse her held her back.

And then he half turned towards her, his hand brushing on hers, but instead of muttered words of contrition and need, it was the plaintive bleat of the communicator in his pocket that filled the waiting silence. 'Saved by the bell,' said Rory in a harsh, humourless voice as he sprang away towards the Range Rover. A moment later, the engine fired and the car raced away towards the town.

Saved by the bell, he had said. Saved from what? A momentary physical impulse only to be bitterly regretted if indulged. What else?

Robin took a deep breath, arranged her face in some sort of serenity and went back to her party.

CHAPTER TEN

ROBIN waved until the ferry with her parents aboard was swallowed up by mist. Then she turned and walked back down the pier in company with a few others brave enough to get up and see the boat away so early on a damp and dismal Monday morning. The Maxwells had taken Dougal with them to finalise the arrangements for his imminent exhibition. So—no parents, no Dougal, no Calum and no Andersons either. Jock, Lindsay and the children were holidaying in Spain.

The Maxwells had enjoyed themselves so much that they had stayed longer than planned and had only gone today because Robin's father was due for a check-up at Edinburgh's famous Royal Alexandra Infirmary tomorrow. The weather had been perfect and being given those few days off was a bonus. At least, her parents had seen it that way. Robin wasn't so sure.

When summoned to Rory's consulting-room two days after her party, she had sped there on winged feet, remembering the atmosphere between them the last time they'd met. But his solemn expression soon extinguished hope. He began by telling her that the laird had made a great improvement over the weekend and now only needed treatment once a day, as a precautionary measure. 'So with pressure relaxed up the hill and some of our outpatients on holiday, it occurred to me that you might wish to take a few days off while your parents are here. Mrs Crawford has amply shown her competence and she is more than willing to stand in for you.'

'Oh, I'm sure she is.'

Robin hadn't meant to sound quite so catty, but she had, and Rory raised an inquisitive eyebrow. 'One would think you resented the chance of a break.' What Robin resented was the feeling of the skids going under, but she forbore to say so in case he confirmed it. 'She could give us Wednesday, Thursday and Friday but not the weekend, having worked this last one,' he had continued, incensing Robin further. Guess who was going to get all the credit for the laird's dramatic recovery—and didn't he realise that she had treated hospital patients almost every weekend since she'd been here?

Robin swallowed hard and said tightly, 'Well, if that suits Mrs Crawford then it has to suit me. And please tell her how much I appreciate her generosity.'

Her irony was wasted. 'Oh, I will,' he had said. 'We have to keep her sweet.'

Robin had left his room on an indrawn breath of exasperation. Couldn't he see what Anne Crawford was up to? Or—nasty thought!—were they both playing the same game?

Going back to work after her mini-break to find her treatment room completely rearranged had infuriated Robin still more. And discovering as she worked that the new arrangement was a great improvement from the time and motion standpoint had been a further irritation.

A sudden vicious gust of rain alerted Robin to the fact that she was getting rather wet and she ran over to her car, parked by the harbour wall. It wasn't worth going back to the cottage, but she was definitely too early for work so she went to the launderette—another of Fergus's many enterprises and very popular with self-catering holiday visitors. There hadn't been time, of course, and she arrived at the Centre ten minutes late. At least there was no sign of the Range Rover but all the same, she had the feeling that it was going to be one of those days.

The morning passed smoothly enough, though, and so did most of the afternoon at the hospital. Then Robin went to treat Mr Stuart-Strang. His chest being better, they were now working on restoring his exercise tolerance. 'I think we might make it to the front door today,' she promised when he had donned dressing-gown and slippers, after fifteen minutes of carefully graded exercise.

'And here was I hoping for a nice walk outside now that it's stopped raining,' he said regretfully.

'All in good time,' promised Robin. He enjoyed his physiotherapy and the main problem was curbing his enthusiasm. Before starting off, she checked his pulse and found it satisfactory. She allowed him a minute or two sitting at the front door to enjoy the view before starting back. They had only gone a step or two before he dropped to the floor without warning and scarcely a sound. In dread, Robin dropped down beside him. He was grey, still—and lifeless.

Oh, God. Cardiac arrest! She yelled for help, then struck his chest a violent blow, but the heart did not respond.

Hand on hand, arms like ramrods—pressing, relaxing, pressing, relaxing . . . Robin shouted again, then gave mouth to mouth breathing. More massage, more breathing, more massage, more breathing—It could only have been a couple of minutes before Ella and Sister Urquhart came running, but to Robin it seemed like half her life.

There came a tiny choking sound, a faint tinge of

pink in the leaden cheeks . . . Robin was crying with relief as the two nurses took over.

When the laird was safely back in bed and attached once more to the little ventilator which had already saved his life once, Ella proposed her favourite remedy for stress—a nice cup of tea. But by then Robin's last outpatients had already been waiting too long and she had to refuse. Speeding down the hill to the Centre, she passed Rory in the Range Rover speeding up.

It was so quiet in the little cottage that evening that Robin couldn't settle. It wasn't just being alone for the first time in a fortnight; her mind kept going back to the events of the afternoon. Everybody knew that cardiac arrest occurred without warning, but had she been pushing him too hard? No. If anything, she'd been holding back. Should she have let him sit looking out like that instead of insisting they returned to the ward? Yet wasn't the logical thing to rest frequently? But it had happened the minute he stood up again. Now just supposing—the sudden drop in blood pressure . . . 'Oh, stop it before you drive yourself crazy,' she heard herself crying out. 'It wasn't your fault. You'd been told to get him going, and that's what you were doing. Besides, you revived him, didn't you?'

But Robin knew she would never be able to sleep without just one more look at him. Snatching up her car keys, she ran outside.

'Right on course,' reported Night Sister reassuringly when Robin asked her how the laird was doing.

'Oh, thank goodness. But could I possibly . . .?'

'See him? Yes of course you can,' Sister nodded understandingly. 'I'd feel exactly the same in your shoes. By the way, congratulations, Robin, you fairly rose to the occasion.'

Robin thanked her and went to see the laird. 'Sleeping like a baby,' whispered his special nurse and reassured by the wave pattern of the oscilloscope, his tranquil appearance and good colour, Robin was just turning to leave when Selina opened the door.

Her expression of anxiety gave way instantly to hatred. 'You!' she hissed with all possible venom. 'I wonder you have the nerve to come near him after what you did today. Get out before I have you thrown out!'

Robin was just too stunned to react, but the nurse dashed forward angrily. 'You'll upset him, going on like that,' she whispered furiously, as she bundled Selina outside. 'Don't you be taking any notice of her,' she whispered kindly to Robin when she returned. 'Miss Selina was never what you could be calling stable and what with her trouble, and now her father being so ill—it's just about unhinged her, I'm thinking.'

'Yes, I suppose so,' Robin managed with a wan little smile of thanks. She was thinking less of Selina's insults, though, than of Nurse's mysterious hint about Selina's trouble. What trouble was that?

Selina herself was in the hall—and so was Rory. So he's still dancing attendance then, thought Robin grimly. Hearing a sound, Selina swung round, then pointed dramatically. 'I want that creature sacked,' she ranted.

'Keep your voice down and don't be absurd! I keep telling you—it was Robin's prompt action that saved your father's life.' He sounded as furious as Selina was.

'Are you mad? She damn nearly killed him!' Her voice rose on a near shriek.

'Don't you realise allegations like that could land you in court if Robin were the vindictive type?' hissed Rory, opening the door of Ella's office with one hand and shoving Selina inside with the other. He swung round and regarded Robin soberly. 'She's hysterical and doesn't know what she's saying,' he said sounding almost apologetic.

Robin agreed with the first bit of the diagnosis, but dismissed the second as the result of blind partiality. 'I might be hysterical myself, were I in the same position,' she allowed.

'Not you.' A tribute to her moral fibre, or an imputation of insensitivity? 'You acted magnificently today and I'll not forget it—but now I have to sort her out.' He went into Ella's room and shut the door. Instantly there was more shouting, then the sound of a slap followed by muffled weeping.

Crying into his shoulder, thought Robin as she trailed dismally down the steps to her car. Right now, I'd give quite a lot for a manly shoulder of my own to cry on. The window of Ella's office was open to the night and Selina's voice floated out, fraught, but clear. 'It's no good. He is going to die—I know it.' A strangled sob. 'Everybody I love dies and leaves me. You won't leave me will you, Rory? Promise! Promise me you'll never leave me.'

There was a long, long moment in which it seemed the world stood still. Then Rory said, 'I haven't stood by you this long to desert you now.'

Robin sagged against her car. Suspicion was bad enough, but while you only suspected, you could also go on hoping you were wrong. But once you knew—really knew, as she did now—then there was nothing left. Vallersay had brought her relief, but only to deal her another, greater blow. She had to leave—and soon. She had a reason; all she needed was an excuse. She hadn't long to wait for that if only she'd known it.

Naturally Robin went first to see the laird next morning,

and was very relieved to discover that he certainly didn't hold her responsible for his near demise the day before. The reactions of all Robin's colleagues also showed that Selina was in a minority of one. Even Netta Drummond sought her out especially to offer her congratulations. How ironic that just as she had made up her mind to leave Vallersay, the last bastion of prejudice should fall.

The hardest thing to bear that day was Rory's praise. He came along to Physio as soon as she got back from the hospital that morning. He spoke with a warmth and sincerity she distrusted, because all the time his words to Selina the night before were echoing in her head. *I haven't stood by you all this time to desert you now.*

'I was only doing what I'd been taught,' she returned quietly when he had done praising her.

'Everybody is taught, but not everybody remembers what to do when the crisis actually occurs. Don't undervalue yourself, Robin.'

Who would have thought in the beginning that one day he would say such a thing to her? She hadn't made the grade with him as a woman, but at least he appreciated her work. 'You're very kind,' she returned stiffly. 'And after all, it is the value other people put on one that really matters.'

'You of all people can't have any cause to complain on that score,' he returned shortly, before turning on his heel and striding out.

Robin stared after him, mystified. What was he getting at now?

The first thing she did on getting home that night was to phone her mother to find out how her father had got on at the hospital that day. 'The news is—not too good, dear,' said her mother, her tone and her words causing

Robin to subside on to the nearest chair. After a
seemingly endless pause, Mrs Maxwell went on, 'As far
I can make out, some of the coronary arteries need
replacing—and very soon. The surgeon can't think how
he has held up for so long. Oh, Robin—I can't take it
in. He's seemed so much better since he retired and we
came home to Scotland.' She gulped. 'Anyway, they
will try to get him in within the fortnight. I know it's
silly, but I do wish you could be here when he—when
they . . .'

'Maybe I can, darling. I'll certainly do my best. But
don't tell Dad or he'll think he's—worse than he is.' If
that were possible. Now it was Robin's turn to swallow
a sob. 'Give him my love . . .' Long before her mother
eventually rang off, Robin had made her plans. They
wouldn't miss her—not now they had the wonderful
Anne Crawford waiting in the wings. In the
circumstances, the Health Board might possibly waive
the usual month's notice and Rory would support that
as he would be so relieved to see her go. What had she
ever been to him but a thorn in his side—one way or
another?

He wasn't free to see her until lunchtime the next day
and by then Robin knew exactly how to put her case
without arousing any suspicion of her own private and
personal reason for going. 'You see, with my sister now
living in Australia, I am the only person my mother can
turn to for support,' she ended, having spelt out the
facts of her father's condition.

Rory had fixed a stony gaze some point beyond her
left shoulder while Robin was speaking. Now his eyes
met hers for a long second before he said heavily, 'It
goes without saying that I am extremely sorry to hear
about your father, but in any case we wouldn't have had
the pleasure of your assistance for very much longer,

would we? Rest assured I shall do all I can to expedite your departure.'

Even though he had only confirmed her suspicion that he secretly wanted her away, Robin still recoiled inwardly from the ease with which he had accepted her news. He hadn't made even a token attempt to persuade her to stay. 'I'm—very grateful,' she mumbled, turning to go.

'Robin!' Hand on the doorknob, she half turned to see him regarding her sternly. 'Just tell me this,' he demanded urgently. 'Was there ever a time, however short, when you felt inclined to stay?'

She stared at him, trying to fathom that. Then with a little shake of her head she answered, 'I don't think so. I believe I always knew that I would be leaving Vallersay sooner or later.'

His expression hardened. 'That is exactly what I thought but I—I wished to have it confirmed. So it only remains for me to hope that—everything will work out well for you.'

'Thank you—as to that, I've always heard that Professor MacFarlane is one of the best. My father is in good hands.'

'You've heard correctly, but my good wishes were intended to be—rather more comprehensive.'

'Thank you very much. I should like to reciprocate,' she returned mechanically.

Rory merely nodded acceptance as she slipped out. What a peculiar end to a rather peculiar conversation, she thought. Anybody would think it was the last they were going to have.

Which in a way it was, because during the time it took to arrange her departure, Rory took care that they were never alone together again. Robin had entertained desperate hopes of her farewell supper party at the

Andersons'—had deliberately walked there, even though it was raining, in case Rory should offer to drive her home. He was called out half-way through and didn't come back.

Robin spent a lot of her remaining spare time revising her records, cleaning all the equipment and preparing helpful notes. Anne Crawford wasn't to have the slightest chance for criticism. The last two or three days raced past with frightening speed and now here she was sailing out of Bratanport on a miserable day just like the one on which she came.

A sob broke in her throat as the last dim outline was swallowed up in mist. She had thought she loved David, but the hurt she had brought to Vallersay had been a pinprick beside the all-pervading hurt she was taking away. It would pass though—it must, or life wouldn't be worth living.

But it didn't. It got worse.

CHAPTER ELEVEN

THE bus home was standing room only as usual, and everybody on it seemed to be racked with winter coughs and sneezes. Robin clung to the handrail and considered another plus of her coming promotion. Parking space was strictly rationed at the Royal Alexandra, but when she was upgraded to assistant head of department in the New Year, she would qualify for a permit and Calum's wee Jap would come into its own again. Careful. Thinking of the boy—newly back in Vallersay and happy once more—usually led her into thinking of others there. And what use was that? Some people got off at the next stop and Robin found herself in a window seat. She cleared the steamy window with the back of her glove and peered out at the people scurrying down the Mound, shoulders hunched against the snell Edinburgh wind.

Across Princes Street, jammed tight with traffic as usual, then northwards through the so-called New Town—actually Georgian—and on to Inverleith. Her parents had sensibly chosen a roomy ground-floor flat in a Victorian villa near the Botanic Gardens. There, hilly up-and-down Edinburgh was reasonably level.

As usual Mrs Maxwell had been listening for Robin's steps on the path and had the front door open before she could get her key in the lock. Robin kissed her mother's cheek and waited for the inevitable, 'How cold you are, darling,' before asking as usual how her father was.

'Fine, fine—we got the length of Stockbridge today along the river, and I was the one who lagged behind.

You've just missed a phone call.'

Robin frowned. 'Not the hospital already?' This was her weekend on.

'No, dear, that nice Mrs Anderson from Bratanport. There! I knew you'd be pleased.' She wasn't wearing her glasses and, missing Robin's expression, had interpreted her sudden gasp as one of pure delight. 'They're in Glasgow, it seems, and she's very keen to hear from you. She left the number—there it is on the pad. You've just got time to call her back while I dish up.'

Mrs Maxwell disappeared kitchenwards, leaving her daughter staring at the phone, frozen in an agony of recollection. At last she recovered enough to dial slowly, willing Lindsay not to mention Rory. 'Robin! Super to hear you. And how come you're still in Edinburgh? But never mind that just now. Jock's at a weekend seminar on obstetrics and I thought, why don't I go too? Last-minute Christmas shopping in the big city and a chance to see Robin can't be bad. So here I am. How are you fixed for tomorrow?'

'Oh, Lindsay—I'm on call this weekend.'

'But you're still allowed to eat, I imagine, so I'll come through on the train and meet you somewhere for lunch. How about that?'

'Wonderful.' They fixed a time for Robin to meet Lindsay at Waverley Station and then Robin said shamefacedly, 'I'm sorry I never got around to answering your last letter.'

'So I should jolly well think, but never mind, I'll forgive you, and we can exchange all our news tomorrow. Jock's still out but he told me I must remember to give you his love.'

'Bless him, and mine to him. Are the children with you?'

'No, Netta's taken them, which is awfully kind of her—

but then she seemed awfully keen for me to come. I don't know why. So it'll just be thee an' me tomorrow, lass.' They talked on until Mrs Maxwell called that dinner was on the table.

Thoughtfully, Robin replaced the receiver. It would be good to see Lindsay again, but did she want to hear everything that Lindsay might have to tell her? Definitely not. Almost she wished that they weren't meeting tomorrow. All the same, Robin took care to be at the station next morning a good ten minutes before Lindsay's train was due.

They met at the barrier and hugged each other and it felt as if they'd last met only yesterday. 'Gosh, it's good to see you, Rob,' enthused Lindsay. 'You've no idea how much I've missed you.'

'Yes, I was a good baby-sitter, wasn't I?' returned Robin, with a pathetic attempt at humour.

'Cheeky!' Lindsay gave her a playful slap. 'You know fine what I mean. Where are we going for lunch? I'm famished.'

'Knowing how you like vegetarian, I thought we'd go to Hamilton's. Besides, they know me there and won't mind taking a call if I'm needed at the hospital.'

The pavements were crowded and there was no chance to do any serious talking until they were seated in a discreet alcove at the popular basement restaurant. There was something Robin was dreading asking, so she got it over at once. 'H-how is—everybody in Vallersay?' Her voice had cracked, causing Lindsay to look at her more carefully than she had so far.

'Nearly everybody is fine, but I'm not so sure about you. You're pounds thinner and looking gey peelie-wally.'

'I've—been rather worried about Dad.'

'Naturally, but didn't you tell me in your first and only letter that he was quite recovered?'

'Yes he is, thank heaven!'

'Yet here you are, still in Edinburgh.' Lindsay put down her fork to lay a sympathetic hand on Robin's wrist. 'It didn't all go wrong again, did it, Rob?'

Robin stared blankly at her across the table. 'What were you meaning?'

'The—er—reunion. With your ex-fiancé.'

'Oh, that. There was no reunion. David seemed to want one but I didn't. I hadn't been long in Vallersay before I realised it was only my pride that had taken a pounding, not my heart.' A shadow flitted across her face as she thought of the man who had shown her the difference, though she'd not realised it at the time. Pull yourself together, Robin. 'But how on earth did you know about that? I certainly never breathed a word to a soul.' But even as she said it, she remembered. So she hadn't been in time to stop her mother telling Netta.

'Well somebody did, dear. You were hardly away before it was all round the island that whenever your father was better, you would be off back to London to marry your David. I thought that must be why we hadn't heard from you—you were too busy getting organised. Then when Dougal McKnight came home last week and told me you had taken a permanent job in Edinburgh, I simply didn't know what to think. So when did you decide you weren't going back to David?'

'As soon as I heard that was what he wanted. My mother told me when they came to stay.'

'Before you resigned, then. So why in the world did you? Surely Rory could have arranged leave of absence for you to come home for your father's op—especially with Dame Anne simply bursting to step in and show us all the ropes. What a female! Still, Rory soon taught her to toe the line.'

Robin's tense expression had relaxed somewhat at

Lindsay's unflattering description of her successor. Now she said quietly, 'That I can well believe, but he was keen enough to have her all the same.'

'Hobson's choice,' returned Lindsay promptly. 'Besides, the horns never came right out until after she was appointed. But you haven't answered my question. Why did you resign?'

Because I love the man who loves Selina Stuart-Strang was the truthful answer, but a girl had her pride. 'I never meant to stay very long. I came to get over David and, having done that—I left. It's as simple as that.'

'Is it really?' commented Lindsay, her eyes now bright with speculation.

Robin had to put a stop to that. 'Everything is going so well for me now, especially job-wise. I'm being made assistant superintendent soon. And I've met up again with friends from my first school—and made a few more. I'm out nearly every night.'

'That must be why you're looking so washed out, then,' returned Lindsay drily. Another shrewd look and then she asked, 'I don't suppose you've met the laird and his lovely daughter during all this racketing around?'

Robin stared. 'Are you telling me they're in Edinburgh?'

'They were, but they may have moved on by now. They're spending Christmas in the south, I believe.' Lindsay took her fork and chased her stuffed aubergine round the plate a bit before proceeding carefully, 'I think Rory was rather relieved. She's been an awful worry to him for some time now.'

'Yes, he's quite devoted to her, isn't he?' If only she'd managed to keep that harsh edge out of her voice!

'Concerned, yes. Devoted—I doubt it.'

'Well, you know him better than I do,' answered Robin, her tone carefully neutral this time, as she ladled sugar she never took into her coffee.

Lindsay watched her with a tiny smile. 'I expect I must do,' she agreed, 'but I seem to be digressing. Such a lot of people asked to be remembered to you.' She reeled off a string of names and in question and answer the rest of the time flew past without any more mention of Rory. They talked for so long that they had to run all the way to the station, or Lindsay would have missed her train.

Waving her friend away, Robin was left with the uncomfortable suspicion that Lindsay had guessed her secret. Her first reaction was anger at having given herself away, but later, as she got off her bus outside the hospital, came the thought that if Rory really was growing tired of Selina then his thoughts might turn to her, Robin, and the good times they had shared. Given that and knowing what she did, Lindsay might contrive to build a bridge . . . Oh, don't be daft, Robin Maxwell! He couldn't get rid of you quickly enough.

Sensibly remembered, but it didn't stop her examining her Christmas mail with much more eagerness than usual. But the days plodded past, and nothing came from Rory.

'I can't tell you how sorry I am about this, Robin,' said the superintendent. 'And on Christmas Eve too—but the girl is really ill.'

'Yes I know and it's quite all right, I wasn't going anywhere special. What about tomorrow and Boxing Day?' Robin pressed on hopefully. 'Andrew won't be able to manage on his own.'

'I'm not allowing you to do all of it, Robin. That would be too much when it's your first family Christmas in Edinburgh for so long.'

'I really wouldn't mind, Mrs Dewar.' Not one little bit, she wouldn't. In fact it would be a great relief to escape from the family party—particularly from Granny Maxwell peering despairingly at her over her glasses all the time and muttering that all her daughters were married and mothers by the time they were Robin's age. Granny at eighty-seven had a one-track mind.

'Robin, you're not listening,' chided the superintendent. 'I was saying that Lorna has offered. She has quarrelled with the boyfriend again and needs something to occupy her mind.'

She's not the only one, thought Robin gloomily, but realising she had been pipped at the post she said, 'As long as we're covered. Goodnight then, Mrs Dewar—and the same to you,' she added in answer to the superintendent's seasonal parting wish. At least she now had an excuse not to go over to Barnton with the parents tonight. Watching nineteen-year-old Cousin Fiona flashing her new diamond solitaire about would be too much. Granny was going to have a field day tomorrow.

Home for an early supper, seeing her parents away entrusted with her rather insincere apologies, and then back to the hospital for two hours of steady slog on the cardio-thoracic unit still left too much time to kill before bedtime. As she let herself into the empty flat Robin was wondering whether to risk washing her hair—she might be called in to an emergency—when the phone rang. She hurried into the hall and picked it up. 'Robin Maxwell, physio on call.'

A slight pause and then, 'So you weren't out at a party after all,' guessed Rory McEwan.

It was a good thing there was a chair handy or Robin would have landed on the floor. 'Good lord,' she breathed after a turbulent, heart-threatening minute.

'And a Merry Christmas to you too. I'm sorry this is such a shock but you have to blame Lindsay. Being all behind with her Christmas mail apparently, she insisted that I delivered her present to you.'

'B-but—where are you?'

'In Edinburgh. Where do you think? I'm not pigeon post.'

'Oh,' was all Robin could manage next. Speech wasn't easy when your heart was in your larynx.

'I could always ring twice like a real postie and leave it on the mat,' he suggested woodenly.

He might have to if she was needed at the hospital, but if that was what he had really intended, wouldn't he have done it by now? 'I'll be here,' she said, defying Providence. 'Do you know the way?'

'I do and, as my friends live in Drummond Place, it shouldn't take more than five minutes.'

Just time to take off her coat, brush her hair, put on some lipstick with a hand that trembled and then coax the damped-down drawing-room fire into a reasonable Yuletide blaze in fact—yet it still seemed an age until the doorbell rang.

Robin flew to open the door—and there he was. In a bulky sheepskin jacket, he seemed to fill the porch. It had started to snow and he was bareheaded. Large wet flakes glistened on his thick brown hair, which needed cutting, thus seeming more untidy than ever. His deep-set grey eyes were watchful and his jawline defensive. 'You're wasting heat,' he observed laconically, sharply reminding her of the time he had told her she needed a new tyre on her car.

She stood aside to let him in, then closed the door. 'Let me take your coat.'

'Am I staying, then?' he asked, but he removed it.

'It's a bit damp. I'll put it in the cloak-room. The central heating boiler is in there, so it'll soon dry.' Stop babbling, she told herself anxiously.

'Like Calum's clothes,' said Rory, watching her. Was that bit of recollection a good or a bad sign?

He still loomed large in the spacious hall and Robin

walked round him to open the drawing-room door. 'It's nice and warm in here. Will you have a drink?'

'A small dram wouldn't come amiss—small, I said,' he added, noting the reckless, or unsteady, way she was dispensing her father's very best malt. 'The polis are out in force tonight and I can't afford to lose my licence.'

It was on the tip of Robin's tongue to say he could always stay the night if necessary, but she didn't. He'd said on the phone he was coming to deliver a parcel and nothing he'd said yet had given her any reason to suppose otherwise. She poured herself some tonic water and sat down on the chesterfield beside the fire. After a moment's hesitation, Rory sat down opposite.

Robin sipped her drink and stared into the fire, finding she couldn't look at him. Only the old carriage clock on the mantelpiece had anything to say for the next long minute. Then Rory said heavily, 'Lindsay says you'll soon be the deputy boss. You've done well.'

'That marvellous reference you gave me helped a lot.'

'You deserved it.' Glass cradled in his hands, he leaned forward, elbows on knees. 'Is that how you see your life going, then?' he demanded.

'For the present, yes. Later—I don't know. My sister keeps asking me to go out and work in Australia for a time.' Surely if he had anything to say to her, that would prompt him.

Rory slumped back in his chair and took a large swig from his glass before saying, 'If you want to travel, then this is probably the best time. Later on, you would have too much seniority to lose.'

Oh, God—she'd miscalculated! Or been too hopeful more likely. 'How's my friend Eorna?' she asked frantically.

'Fine. Netta and Archie are looking after her over the holiday.'

'You're spending Christmas in Edinburgh, then?'

'Didn't I say so?'

'No, I don't think you did.'

'Well, I am.' He sounded almost truculent.

There was another awkward pause. In desperation Robin got up and went over to the drinks cupboard to splash more tonic in her glass. She held out the whisky decanter. 'A top-up?'

'No, thanks.' Rory got up too and crossed over to plant himself firmly in front of her. 'I suppose you know that even before you left, there was a rumour going round that you were getting married?'

'Lindsay did mention it. I think it must have been something misleading my mother said.'

'Which is probably why—everybody believed it.'

'I suppose so. Mother would certainly have liked me to make it up with David, only by then—by then I knew I didn't love him and probably never had.'

'And what brought you to that conclusion?'

Robin stopped trying to pleat her handkerchief and faced him directly for the first time since that moment on the doorstep. 'I forgot him too easily.'

'You certainly had plenty of help.' His tone was bitter.

'Dougal and Fergus, you mean, I suppose. Well—so did you,' she retaliated.

Rory came a step nearer, scowling. 'Meaning what?'

'Selina and me—after Deirdre. Oh, yes, Dougal told me all about her. Pots shouldn't miscall kettles,' she wound up, scowling herself.

'There's absolutely no parallel,' he grated.

'Now where have I heard that before?' wondered Robin sarcastically as his hands descended with a vice-like grip on her shoulders.

'God, but you're mixed up,' he said between clenched teeth. 'Now listen. You're not the only one who can make mistakes and Deirdre was the biggest one I ever made. She was totally self-centred, and not much good at her job either. It was more of a relief than anything when she took herself off. Not that anybody would have believed me if I'd said so. They'd merely have thought I was saving face.'

That figured. 'And Selina?'

'Well, what about her?'

'She's—very beautiful.'

'Yes, isn't she? She's also as unstable as a cartload of weasels. My cousin must have been out of his skull to think of marrying her.'

His cousin? This was a new twist. 'I hadn't heard about that,' she murmured thoughtfully.

'No? Certainly the islanders, though ready enough to gossip among themselves, are canny enough with outsiders—but I'd have thought something like that would have filtered through.'

'Did he—break it off, then?' she prompted.

'He died.' Abruptly he let her go.

'Oh, I'm so sorry.' Robin would have given anything to have taken back her question.

'Actually he was killed,' Rory went on, staring moodily into space. 'Jamie and I used to go climbing together and we'd planned to do the Caisteal ridge that weekend, but I had to cry off for an emergency. He insisted on going alone and—the mist came down. He fell and was critically injured.' He swallowed visibly. 'We—weren't able to save him.'

'Oh, Rory, how awful!' She laid a hand on his sleeve and he didn't shrug it off.

'I honestly believe Selina loved him as much as she could love anyone, and she nearly went mad. Threw all sorts of wild accusations about—the way she did when her father had his cardiac arrest. Even though the accident was not my fault, I still felt partly responsible. After all, it was

I who taught Jamie to climb—and not well enough, apparently. Anyway, I propped her up for longer than I should have and she came to expect I always would.'

'If only I'd known,' she whispered. 'Why didn't you tell me?'

'Apart from thinking you must know, you never seemed to—to care.' His voice broke.

'Oh, Rory . . .' The hurt in his eyes was too much to take and Robin slid her arms tightly round him, pressing her face in his shoulder just as his arms closed round her. They stood in silence for a long time, holding each other more and more closely, as reassurance and understanding flowed between them at last.

'People seem to think it's a picnic falling in love,' murmured Rory at length. 'But it isn't—it's damn difficult and very painful. We met too soon after our mistakes and didn't dare trust our senses. I'd given you every cause to dislike me, too, and then other people kept getting in the way. We needed time, *mo gràdh*, and time was something we just didn't have.'

'Everything is all right now,' she murmured soothingly against his cheek.

'But is it?' Suddenly she was at arm's length again as Rory's eyes bored anxiously into hers. 'You're not an islander. Vallersay in winter might drive you nuts. We were cut off for ten days last month when the ferry couldn't get into the pier for the storms. I'm not going to risk it. It might take a bit of time, but I'm fairly sure I can get back on the circuit in Glasgow.'

'Would you really do that—for me?'

'For us both. If you were unhappy I don't think I could bear it.'

'I can be happy anywhere you are, my love,' she crooned.

'Even in Vallersay?'

'Especially in Vallersay,' she insisted just before his mouth closed on hers again.

The cure had worked—and how!

Hello!

As a reader, you may not have thought about trying to write a book yourself, but if you have, and you have a particular interest in medicine, then now is your chance.

We are specifically looking for new writers to join our established team of authors who write Medical Romances. Guidelines are available for this list, and we would be happy to send them to you.

Please mark the outside of your envelope 'Medical' to help speed our response, and we would be most grateful if you could include a stamped self-addressed envelope, size approximately $9\frac{1}{4}''$ x $4\frac{3}{4}''$, sent to the address below.

We look forward to hearing from you.

Editorial Department,
Mills & Boon Limited,
Eton House,
18-24 Paradise Road,
Richmond, Surrey,
TW9 1SR.

THE IDEAL TONIC

New Beginnings — ANN JENNINGS

A Stormy Partnership — KATHLEEN FARRELL

Misplaced Loyalty — JENNY ASHE

Over the past year, we have listened carefully to readers' comments, and so, in August, Mills & Boon are launching a *new look* Doctor-Nurse series – MEDICAL ROMANCES.

There will still be three books every month from a wide selection of your favourite authors. As a special bonus, the three books in August will have a special offer price of **ONLY** 99p each.

So don't miss out on this chance to get a real insight into the fast-moving and varied world of modern medicine, which gives such a unique background to drama, emotions – and romance!

Widely available from Boots, Martins, John Menzies, W.H. Smith, Woolworths and other paperback stockists.
Usual price £1.25

THE COMPELLING
AND UNFORGETTABLE SAGA OF
THE CALVERT FAMILY

| April | August | November |
| **£2.95** | **£3.50** | **£3.50** |

From the American Civil War to the outbreak of World War I, this sweeping historical romance trilogy depicts three generations of the formidable and captivating Calvert women – Sarah, Elizabeth and Catherine.

The ravages of war, the continued divide of North and South, success and failure, drive them all to discover an inner strength which proves they are true Calverts.

Top author Maura Seger weaves passion, pride, ambition and love into each story, to create a set of magnificent and unforgettable novels.

W❍RLDWIDE

Widely available on dates shown from Boots, Martins, John Menzies, W.H. Smith, Woolworths and other paperback stockists.

FRUIT SALAD WORDSEARCH
COMPETITION!

How would you like a years supply of Mills & Boon Romances ABSOLUTELY FREE? Well, you can win them! All you have to do is complete the word puzzle below and send it in to us by Dec. 31st. 1989. The first 5 correct entries picked out of the bag after that date will win **a years supply of Mills & Boon Romances** (*ten books every month - worth £162*) What could be easier?

```
T E T A N A R G E M O P
A N E Y E P A R G A A E
N E A R S P I M N N T A
G N P R T L W E A D Y C
E I R E R E I L R A R H
R R I B A U K O O R R M
I A C P W R C N O I E A
N T O S B A R K E N H N
E C T A E E F R C U C A
I E T R R P O G N A M N
T N A R R U C D E R L A
E E H C Y L L E M O N B
```

RASPBERRY	ORANGE	LYCHEE
REDCURRANT	MANGO	CHERRY
BANANA	LEMON	KIWI
TANGERINE	APRICOT	GRAPE
STRAWBERRY	PEACH	PEAR
POMEGRANATE	MANDARIN	APPLE
BLACKCURRANT	NECTARINE	MELON

PLEASE TURN OVER FOR DETAILS ON HOW TO ENTER

HOW TO ENTER

All the words listed overleaf, below the word puzzle, are hidden in the grid. You can find them by reading the letters forward, backwards, up or down, or diagonally. When you find a word, circle it or put a line through it, the remaining letters (which you can read from left to right, from the top of the puzzle through to the bottom) will spell a secret message.

After you have filled in all the words, don't forget to fill in your name and address in the space provided and pop this page in an envelope (you don't need a stamp) and post it today. Hurry - competition ends December 31st. 1989.

Mills & Boon Competition,
FREEPOST,
P.O. Box 236,
Croydon,
Surrey. CR9 9EL

Only one entry per household

Secret Message _____

_____

Name _____

Address _____

_____

_____

_____ Postcode _____

You may be mailed as a result of entering this competition
Please tick the box if you are a Reader Service subscriber ☐

COMP7